Praise for Cindy Procter-King

"Simply enchanting!"

— InD'tale Magazine on BEFORE
BRADY

"What a set-up for a comedy of errors! Everything that can go wrong in this scenario does go wrong, and the reader is well entertained by the comedic chaos."

— Fallen Angel Reviews on HEAD
OVER HEELS

"I really enjoyed *Borrowing Alex*. It was smart and funny without being overdone. The characters do some pretty funny things in the name of love. I am definitely looking forward to reading the next book I find by Cindy Procter-King."

— Joyfully Reviewed on BORROWING
ALEX

"I really like romantic comedy as a genre, but it takes some really good writing to make me laugh. This book made me laugh."

> — Fallen Angel Reviews on
> BORROWING ALEX

"'*Getting Over Brett*' is everything a romantic comedy should be!...a very funny, light and easy romance that will leave a big goofy smile on your face!"

> — InD'tale Magazine on GETTING
> OVER BRETT

"*Getting Over Brett* is a top-of-the-line read. It has everything you could possibly want in a modern romance. It's fun and playful at times, full of flirty banter, then deeply romantic and emotional at its heart. Somehow, it's both sweet and sexy all at the same time!"

> —Julianne MacLean, USA Today
> Bestselling Author

"Cindy Procter-King presents readers with a suspenseful snapshot of a romantic comedy... loaded with humor, this is a must-read."

— Night Owl Reviews on PICTURE IMPERFECT

"Procter-King has written a 'home' for all of us. Destiny Falls is the place that holds your first love, your first triumph..."

— RT Book Reviews on WHERE SHE BELONGS

Trusting Trey

Also by Cindy Procter-King

Steamy RomCom

Love & Other Calamities

RomCom Series

Deceiving Derek (Book 1)

Catching Claire (Book 2)

Before Brady (Book 3)

Just Janie (Book 4)

Love in the Pacific Northwest

Stand-alone Romantic Comedy

Head Over Heels (Book 1)

Borrowing Alex (Book 2)

Getting Over Brett (Book 3)

Contemporary Romance

Single Title Romance

Picture Imperfect (Sassy Mystery Romance)

Where She Belongs (Emotional Small Town Romance)

Trusting Trey

CINDY PROCTER-KING

Blue Orchard Books

TRUSTING TREY

Copyright © 2025 Cindy Procter-King

All rights reserved.

No part of this publication maybe be reproduced in any form or by any electronic or mechanical means, including information storage and retrieval systems, or otherwise, without explicit written permission from the author, except in the case of brief quotations used in book reviews and articles.

This is a work of fiction. Characters, names, places, events, incidents, scenarios, opinions, brands, media, are of the author's imagination or are used fictitiously. Any resemblance to actual incidents, locales, or persons, living or dead, is entirely coincidental.

Trusting Trey © 2025 by Cindy Procter-King

Published by Blue Orchard Books

Cover by The Killion Group

ISBN: 978-1-989113-04-2 (eBook)

ISBN: 978-1-989113-09-7 (Print)

For my mom. I love you.

Chapter One

Saturday morning, July 29th
Countdown to Tania and Trey's wedding: Today
(unless...)

Tania Hoyt dry-heaved into the toilet, elbows digging into the porcelain edges of the bowl and the heels of her palms kneading her temples.

Oh. My. Mother-fluffer.

Fingers tangling in the thick strands of light red hair hanging down on either side of her face, Tania inhaled on a fatigued gasp. Not one speck of her paltry breakfast...nor a dollop of orange juice...not even a metallic-tasting ounce of bile remained in her stomach. The queasiness that had intensified over the last week, advancing and retreating with no regard to her planned-to-the-minute wedding-day countdown, refused to subside.

If anything, the seasickness-like spells were getting worse.

"Cold feet," she mumbled, voice echoing in the empty bathroom. "It's nothing more than a case of chilly toes." She stared into the bowl. But—she swallowed past the lump in her throat—*was it?*

A sense of doom wriggled beneath her skin and thrashed about like a caged rattlesnake, hardly the emotion she'd expected to encounter on today of all days, her wedding to the most amazing man in the world. Her senses of taste and smell had propelled into mutant territory. Not the sexy mutants found in comics, TV, and movies, either. Nope, she had transformed into an unappealing, walking, talking, and far-too-emotional bundle of nerves. Complete with over-the-top olfactory and gustatory systems.

"Pull it together, Nearly Mrs. Whitaker," she whispered, rocking back on her bare feet. Her heels, pumiced to perfection yesterday, remained tucked beneath the satin rose-gold nightie and dressing gown covering her butt. "Trey doesn't want to marry a basket case." Closing her eyes, she pushed a shoulder-length strand of hair off her cheek and rested her hands on the slippery fabric draping her thighs. She focused on her breathing. "I am calm. I am in control. I am unflustered."

Tania grimaced. *Hah.* She was anything *but* unflustered.

Lids shut, she pictured her fiancé standing at the church altar at four this afternoon, love and the stalwart devotion she treasured shining in his hazel eyes. Inhaling to a slow count of five and exhaling to a tally of six, she imagined Trey's solid embrace, the tender brushing of his lips on hers, the way they balanced each other, her yin to his yang. She pictured his dark-blond hair, cut fuller in front and cropped on the sides, his tidy beard, handsome features, and the cute ears that stuck out a quarter inch too far.

She wouldn't have his ears—or him—any other way.

"I am calm." A palm to her breastbone, she breathed in through her nostrils. "I am composed." Like Trey.

In a matter of hours, she would tie the knot with her fiancé of two years and boyfriend of four. She had expected nerves as the big day approached. In point of fact, she had researched bridal jitters to death. The unending horrors of recent wedding-planning catastrophes were responsible for the itch tingling between her shoulder blades and the invisible eels swimming in her belly. The universe *wasn't* trying to send her a message that she should cut and run. And not marry Trey—for his own good.

A sheen of perspiration dampened her forehead. She wiped a shaking hand across her brow. This was ridiculous!

She bent over the toilet again, stomach cramping.

Damn it, if her mother or one of her sisters caught her praying to the Great Porcelain Deity on the morning of her wedding, she would never live it down.

Getting up, she flushed the toilet's contents into the void of the efficient plumbing in her mother's immaculate French provincial house. Washed her hands and face. Brushed her teeth. Squared her shoulders.

Opening vanity cabinets, she searched for a bottle of tablets or bright pink medicinal goop to settle her tummy. Last night, one whiff of the bacon-wrapped mushrooms served at the rehearsal dinner almost made her hurl onto Trey's crisp white dress shirt.

Her fingers bumped a package toward the rear of

the highest shelf. Holding her breath, she extracted the box. Then gawped at the logo. *A pregnancy test?*

Tania met her wide-eyed gaze in the mirror. Who had hidden a pregnancy test in the second-floor bathroom she currently shared with her two younger sisters?

Had it been Tami? Or Noni?

Her stomach pitched.

"Take the test," her reflection whispered.

She shook her head.

Take the test, an inner voice commanded.

At least she *hoped* it was an inner voice and not another sign out of the dozens this summer that she was losing her ever-loving mind.

"No." She wagged a finger at her reflection. "*No.*" She stamped a foot on the cool tiles. She would not entertain the notion of an *unplanned* pregnancy. She taught middle-school biology. She knew better. She and Trey had been so careful. They hadn't made love in a little over two weeks, not since the morning she'd moved out of their old apartment. The transition occurred a couple of days before her second bridal shower, which had quickly escalated into a wild bachelorette party.

Omigod, the bachelorette party! Tania's fingers flew to her suddenly hot cheeks.

"You *weren't* sloshed at the party," she reminded herself, pointing at her mirror image. Although, she had let her friends believe she was overboard tipsy. True, she had polished off the first of the creamy drinks her maid of honor had concocted. But then she'd sipped at and secretly poured the others down the sink. Her friends had outdone themselves organizing a fun night, and she'd wanted everyone to have a good time. As she'd realized thirty minutes into the festivities, their definition of fun included getting the bride pie-eyed. The cocktails hadn't ticked off the boxes on her strict wedding-gown diet, so down the sink they'd disappeared. Thank God.

Forehead furrowing, she counted back the weeks of her cycle on her thumb. Usually, she and Trey shared a passion for amorous action. This summer had been different. The stress of wedding planning had occupied her every waking moment. Except for—

Her heart sank. Her reflection paled.

That romantic night in mid-June. Beneath the light of a full moon.

Oh, no. Oh, no, no, no. Slapping her forehead, she hopped up and down. It couldn't be.

She counted on her fingers again. *Mother-fluffer!*

Not the *one single solitary time* she'd forgotten to pack her pills for some much-needed couple time away from Rosewood, at the Whitakers' family oceanfront vacation property on Bainbridge Island. She hadn't been able to resist the sensual pleasure of Trey's lips on hers as they'd lowered onto the soft cushions and woven blankets scattered beneath the copper patio heaters on the huge cedar deck. Even in June, following a day of sprinkling rain, the heaters provided a cozy atmosphere.

But she and her fiancé weren't stupid. They'd taken *other* precautions. Still, mistakes happened.

Tania should know. She was a mistake.

"It's just a stick," she whispered to her stricken reflection. "Pee on it. Get some answers." Fingers trembling, she opened the box and shook out the crinkly cylindrical wrapper covering the test. She unfolded the directions onto the counter.

A loud knock bashed the door. The pregnancy test launched out of her hands and landed in the sink.

"Tania," her youngest sister yelled from the hall. "Come downstairs. Quick." The privacy lock rattled.

"Noni? What on earth?" Tania snatched the covered test and zipped the crinkly cylinder inside her bridal makeup bag. "Why the rush?" she asked, buying time as she flattened the box and buried the packaging and directions in the bottom of a magazine drawer. "Last I checked, it was ten to nine." Hours until her family needed to leave the house.

Another loud rap echoed throughout the bathroom. "You have a delivery."

"Can't someone else sign for it?"

"Not this time. You're so lucky."

Tania nibbled her lip. Another gift from Trey? He was spoiling her, and she wasn't sure she deserved it.

She opened the door.

Noni, wearing PJ pants and a baggy T-shirt, grabbed Tania's hand and yanked her at a breakneck pace toward the stairs.

Keeping an eye on the gray haze of smoke in the overcast morning sky twenty miles west, Trey Whitaker downshifted his BMW coupe and steered into his future mother-in-law Bea Hoyt's ritzy neighborhood. He didn't want Bea's daughter—*his* fiancée—hearing the news from anyone else.

Tania would flip a totally understandable lid.

They weren't getting married today.

At least, not in the historic wooden church she had her heart set on.

Frowning as he caught sight of a commotion several yards ahead, he parked at the sidewalk bordering the manicured front lawn and stared out the windshield. Throwing up his hands, he appealed to the wedding gods. "What now?"

Tania stood in the patterned-concrete driveway, along with her mom and her youngest sister. Wearing flip-flops on her bare feet, she adjusted the sash of a long pink bathrobe. As usual, love radiated from his chest upon spotting her. But he couldn't indulge in romanticisms now. Her back to the ashes blurring the horizon, she stared at the vehicle-delivery truck unloading her surprise wedding present. *Three damn hours early.* Two delivery guys monitored the truck's progress.

Unbuckling his seatbelt, Trey groaned. Would nothing go their way today? Like Tania's dog and her mother's cat not seeing eye to eye—again?

"Argh, probably not," he grumbled, scraping a hand over his beard and climbing out of the car.

He slipped his keys into a pocket of his rehearsal-dinner dress pants and smoothed the wrinkles from his *Last Chance for Bromance* golf shirt. After reading a report about the fire online, he'd immediately thrown on the nearest clothes and driven across town. The last thing he needed was another bunch of complications plaguing preparations for his and Tania's wedding scheduled for this afternoon. Now, on this last Saturday of July, he once again needed to call on his bride-to-be to keep the faith. Not only in him, but in what they meant to each other and the life they would build together.

He refused to lose the woman he loved to the pressure-filled spectacle their wedding had become.

Pasting on a smile, he strode toward the driveway. "Tania," he called, waving as the delivery team wheeled the white sports car of her dreams off the ramp. "Happy wedding day, babe."

"*Trey?*" Her hand flew up, shielding her gaze like the bill of a baseball cap. "Oh, my God, honey. What are you doing here? I can't see you! It's bad luck."

"Superstition," Trey rationalized, praying he was right. As she had reminded him on multiple occasions, wedding tradition stipulated that they weren't to catch a glimpse of each other until she walked down the now-non-existent church aisle with her mom.

Reaching for her, he grasped her arms. The silky fabric of her dressing gown slid beneath his fingertips. "Tania. Please. I need to tell you something ."

"About the car?" She blinked and gestured to the burgundy soft-top of the convertible. "It's gorgeous, Trey," she breathed. "But really, it's too much. I mean, it's not the right time. I mean—"

Noni, Tania's youngest sister, piped up. "She's a little tongue-tied. What I'm sure my sister means to say is, your gift arrived, and it's beautiful. Thank you. Full stop."

"The car is lovely," Tania's mom agreed, a smile on her face. Bea placed a hand on the casual top covering her chest. "You're such a gentleman," she murmured.

Trey glanced at Bea. Then Noni. A whisper of relief washed through him.

They don't know about the fire. Yet.

Which meant Tania didn't know yet, either.

All four Hoyt women wore their hearts on their sleeves. At times, their spirited reactions to situations intimidated others, but Trey had known this family for years. Before the day was through, Tania's family would become *his* family. He would do anything for every one of them.

"Tania," he whispered, kissing his five-foot-two-inch-tall fiancée's forehead. He brushed soft wisps of her lustrous copper-penny hair off her face. Even considering the upsetting news he needed to divulge, he couldn't stop the smile tugging at his lips. Tania was his heart. She had stood by him during a major career sideswipe, and she would stand by him again today. Of that, he was certain.

She peeked up, and her rosy lips parted. Worry reflected in the soft green of her cat's eyes.

He stifled a curse. Had he messed up with the car? Was it the wrong color? He tucked his bride beneath his arm. "This is your wedding present, sweetheart." He spread a hand toward the small white car.

"And I love it, but...it only has two seats." Her voice squeaked. A glistening tear spilled over her fair lashes and trickled down her cheek.

"Aw, babe." Chest squeezing, he brushed away the dampness with his thumbs. "It's the model we test-drove in May." During a spontaneous visit to the dealership following a laughter-filled afternoon at a park. Had he miscalculated, purchasing the lavish gift? "You said you yearned for this car, if I remember correctly," he reminded Tania in a gentle tone, caressing her shoulder. "It fills me with happiness thinking about you and Teacup motoring around our new neighborhood in this beauty when I need to go out of town." A trusted dog sitter would care for their miniature Yorkshire terrier until they returned from honeymoon. The last-minute change from their original plans for Teacup to stay with Tania's mom had been another in a long string of stressful adjustments. Trey asked, "Can't you picture Tea-baby riding shotgun in a wine-colored pet carrier, a matching hairbow in her fancy updo?"

She flinched at his endearment for the dog. "Tea*cup*," she whispered, emphasizing the second syllable. "Our dog's name is Teacup."

His lips quirked. "You call her Tea-baby half the time."

"Yeah, but she's not human. I mean—" She sucked in air. "Trey. I love you so much. And I adore the car. I do. It's just a lot to take in." One of her hands fluttered to the sash of the dressing gown cinched at her trim waist.

"The spontaneity makes it fun." He paused, palm on her shoulder. "We can send it back." He held his breath as her uncertain gaze traveled over the car. He would have bought the perky roadster on the spot in the wake of their impromptu test drive, but his schoolteacher fiancée had said that after spending a "small fortune" on their wedding, which she had mainly planned on her own, as well as investing in a luxury condo to begin their married lives, they should wait to update her sky-blue sedan in need of repairs.

The thing was, money was the least of their concerns. Last fall, Trey's uncles sold Whitaker Organic Farms—a thriving multigenerational business—to a California conglomerate. His father, the youngest of three sons, hadn't supported the decision. Several tense discussions between the senior Whitaker family members had ensued.

Trey hadn't been thrilled about the sale, although he understood his uncles' reasons. His dad, himself, and his younger brother Heath had reaped the financial benefits of working for Whitaker Organic Farms throughout their lives, and the sale had fattened their wallets. In the end, Trey's dad succumbed to the appeal of early retirement while Heath realized a long-held dream of opening a skateshop. Meanwhile, Trey was tapped to oversee Whitaker family interests throughout the transition. His contract with the California firm ended this October. *Then* he would finally get the chance to pursue *his* dream of opening a consulting business helping Washington farmers wanting to make the move to organic as independents.

A plan in place, his future excited him. Especially

because Tania supported his giant leap into the unknown.

He rubbed her shoulder again. "Should we send back the car?" he whispered near her ear. "Just say the word."

"Uh, no. Not yet. Maybe not at all." Her smile wobbled. "It's not a decision I feel prepared to make right now. Trey, I'm sorry. We've had a lot of surprises this summer."

"I hear you." Unfortunately, he was about to unleash another mother of a shocker to her system. He stole a glance at the sky behind the house. To his amazement, none of the Hoyt women noticed the smoky haze fanning the gauzy cloud cover. Granted, the church sat—*had* sat—twenty miles away. Still, unless his imagination worked overtime, an odor of musty fireplaces tickled his nostrils.

He motioned a hand toward the delivery team. "I'll handle the paperwork. Then we'll talk." About a lot more than her new car.

Tania nodded. Mouth twisting as she chewed the inside of her cheek, she stepped to the roadster and skimmed a palm over the hood. She sighed as if in love with the vehicle already. Her mom and sister circled around her and oohed.

Trey headed for the delivery guy gripping a clipboard a dozen feet away. The second man climbed into the cab of the rollback truck.

Trey scanned the clipboard fellow's name tag. "Barry? That you?"

"Yup." Barry yawned and passed over the paperwork.

Trey examined the documents. "What went wrong here, Barry?" He looked up. "The instructions clearly state a noon delivery."

"Meh." Barry shrugged. "It's a mess downtown, what with the—"

"Don't say it," Trey warned. "It's our wedding day."

"Really?" Barry peered Tania's direction. She strolled around the roadster in her flip-flops, expression thoughtful and arms crossed. "At the old church?" Barry asked.

Trey signed the documents. "Yep."

Barry whistled through his teeth. "That's rough. What can I say, buddy? Considering the...event, it was deliver the car now or wait until Monday."

"Monday doesn't work. We'll be on our honeymoon."

"The boss said now." Barry gave another shrug.

Trey returned the clipboard. "Next customer, try

emailing or sending a text message first. Or, I don't know, how about a phone call?"

"I'll pass on the feedback." Barry tore off a perforated sheet and handed the paper to Trey, along with a key fob. "Better tell the ladies about the church," Barry advised, slipping the clipboard beneath one arm. He ambled toward the rollback truck.

"That's why I'm here," Trey mumbled. He folded the document into a pocket and slipped the keys into another. The space in his pockets was growing scarce.

Raking a hand through his hair, he faced the three women as the truck rumbled down the street. He crooked a finger. "Tania?" The sooner he delivered his wretched news about the church, the sooner they could proceed toward finding solutions.

His fiancée's head swung toward him. Just then, Tami, her middle sister, burst through the elegant double front doors of the house. Clad in a housecoat, a false eyelash clinging to a cheek and a pair of women's fancy white high heels dangling from her fingers, Tami careened down the walkway.

Bea's hands shot to her hips. "*Tamsin Wynette. What on earth?*"

Tami skidded to a stop. "Mr. Sprinkles strikes again!"

Chapter Two

Tania stiffened as a sensation akin to a bucket of ice cubes tumbling over her scalp chilled her skin. She stared at Tami. "What's this about the cat?" she asked, struggling to contain the alarm clambering up her throat. She hadn't yet processed Noni's interruption in the bathroom. Plus, the perky sports car parked at the curb of her mother's house had knocked her for a loop. She desperately craved a few minutes of privacy to complete the drugstore test and decide if she should ask Trey to replace his generous gift with a minivan. And now Tami was blathering about their mom's pet?

Tania's gaze caught on the beaded wedding sandals swaying in her younger sister's shaking hands. "Tami, why do you have my shoes?" Tania caught the stilettos as they toppled from Tami's grasp.

Tami sputtered. "I—I—"

Noni's eyes bugged. "Cat spray? Not again."

Trey ran a finger across his whiskered upper lip. "You have got to be kidding me," he muttered.

Mom lowered her nose to the sandals and sniffed. "It's not cat spray," she declared. Pursing her lips, Mom glanced around the front yard. A furrow plowed a trench between her eyebrows.

The comforting weight of Trey's hand settled on Tania's shoulder. She tried to focus on the warmth of his touch. Fought to prevent her potentially hormonal disappointment from bubbling forth. But another glance at her wedding shoes ground her efforts into sand.

"They're ruined," she cried out. Her fingertips traveled over the bumpy rips in the bedazzled satin. "Mr. Sprinkles clawed them up." What other explanation was there? Pushing the pregnancy scare to the back of her mind, she focused on the immediate problem. Six days ago, last weekend, Mr. Sprinkles stress-sprayed the centerpieces for tonight's wedding reception. It made sense that the frustrated feline had continued his vengeful reign of terror on her shoes.

Inhaling deeply, she willed a sense of calm to enter her being. Since the centerpiece debacle, she understood that her mom's cat didn't bear ill will toward Teacup. Or toward *her*. Or Trey. Or their wedding. After all, Mr. Sprinkles and Tania's darling Yorkie rarely encountered each other. Or that *was* the case before she and the dog moved into her old bedroom for the half-month preceding the wedding. During previous family gatherings, Tania had either left Teacup at home or Mr. Sprinkles hid beneath Mom's living room couch.

Apparently, Mr. Sprinkles hadn't considered it prudent to slink behind the furniture for fourteen days. Removing the dog from the premises had seemed best. Trey's brother stepped up, arranging alternate Yorkie care. But this—*this*—this business with her wedding shoes was another matter!

She glared at her middle sister. "Tami, how did this happen? These shoes were *boxed*." Inside a locked closet.

Tami's eyebrows arched. "Don't shoot the messenger." The false eyelash sticking to her cheek wiggled loose and fluttered onto the driveway. "I saw the box on Noni's bed. Her door was open."

Noni gnawed a fingernail. "I might've taken the shoes out of the wedding closet." She winced. "Then out of the box. For a minute. Maybe twenty. To admire them. And try them on. They're a little small for me. In the middle of everything, I got hungry. I ran down to the kitchen for some yogurt. I thought the cat was outside, I swear." She placed a hand over her heart. "Tania, you gotta admit, these sandals are way nicer than mine. And Tami's. And the sandals of every bridesmaid." Noni's gaze lowered to the ruined shoes. "Well, they *were* nicer."

Tania gritted her teeth and stamped her foot. "That's because I'm the bride!" She walked in circles with her hands in her hair.

"The sandals were a temptation," Noni said. "That's all I'm saying."

Stopping, Tania gave her head a curt shake. "My point stands. I'm the bride, Noni, not you." Honestly, if their mother hadn't petitioned her to include both sisters in the wedding party, she wouldn't need to deal with this sibling-rivalry nonsense. The addition had increased the numbers to five attendants per side, as well as a cousin's cute kids taking part as flower girl and ring bearer. Tania had wanted her three closest friends as bridesmaids, and no more. In the end, she'd agreed. Family was family. Where her mom and sisters were concerned.

The pressure of Trey's hand on her rigid

shoulder muscles increased a fraction, their signal that she might be approaching Bridezilla Zone.

Tami shrugged. "It feels like bad luck, wearing clawed shoes for your wedding."

"No *duh*." Tania stared at her sister. It felt like horrible luck. She felt like she starred in a distorted version of Cinderella...or...or was this business with the shoes yet another sign she and Trey weren't meant to tie the knot today, regardless of the results of the pregnancy test? She swallowed. *Please, not that.*

Mom's fingertips fluttered toward Tami. "Don't be silly, Tams. Tania will wear your sandals."

Tami's mouth dropped open.

Mom continued, "No one will look at your feet, Tamsin. You and Tania wear the same size. Winona's feet are one size larger."

Noni wrapped her arms around her waist and scraped a flip-flop against the driveway. "It's not my fault I wanted to try on the prettiest sandals—"

"It *is* your fault," Trey stated, eyes hard as stone. "But Tania and I have bigger concerns than replacing her wedding shoes."

Tania resisted the impulse to widen her gaze. *Little does he know.*

Mom's nostrils flared. "What's that stench?"

Tania sniffed the air. "You're right. It smells like camping in a downpour." She and Trey were camping two states away for their honeymoon, away from this madness. She couldn't wait.

His thumb caressed the back of her neck. His ability to remain composed under nearly any circumstances centered her.

"There was a fire," he said. "In the middle of town." He pointed to the grayish skies behind the house.

"A fire?" Tania parroted as she, her mom, and her sisters all turned. They gawked at the ashen canopy billowing above Rosewood. *"Oh, no."* Her pregnancy worries receded. She *would* deal with the test. Later. "Those poor people. Was it a business?"

Noni dragged a phone out of a pocket of her PJ pants. Trey covered the screen with a hand. "Not now," he said kindly.

Blinking, Noni put away the phone.

Tania's heartbeat pounded in her ears. "T-Trey?" Her throat dried.

His reassuring gaze met hers. "It'll be okay," he said in a soothing voice. His glance moved to encompass her mom and sisters. He extricated the cat-clawed sandals from her stiff fingers and arranged the footwear on the trunk of the sports car. He clasped her hands within his larger ones. The warmth of his touch heated her skin. "We five," he said, meeting her gaze before looking at her family members, "are one of four unfortunate groups affected by today's events. Add on the minister and the members of the congregation, and so on, and so forth."

Tania shook her head. "Because of a business fire? What do you mean?"

Trey's voice softened and lowered. "A blaze broke out around three this morning." He waited a beat. "In the church hall."

"The hall?" she whispered, eyebrows jumping.

He nodded. "The flames leaped to the church in the unpredictable way fires do."

Tania lifted trembling fingers to her mouth. "Please say the flames didn't damage the exterior," she whispered with an utter lack of hope.

He cleared his throat. "They did."

"Trey." She squeezed his hands. "Tell me."

He inhaled. "From what I caught online before I left our old place, the fire began in the hall or a shop on the other side of the building. At any rate, the damage spread to the outside of the church. *And* the inside. Love, another wedding won't occur at Rosewood Community Church until it's rebuilt. Which will take months. Maybe longer."

His words reverberated in her ears, but her brain refused to connect the dots. "But we aren't getting married in the hall," she blurted, even as she realized her comment didn't compute. Neither were they holding their reception in the neighborhood. She'd booked a ballroom at the hotel lodging their out-of-town guests. Only their ceremony had been slated for the old church.

She placed a hand on her gurgling tummy. She had always dreamed of exchanging vows at the historic site where her grandparents started their happy marriage. She yearned to emulate their success, not start married life surrounded by turmoil.

In contrast, her parents were married at a Las Vegas wedding chapel when she was two years old, and her mother was seven months pregnant with Tami. The newlyweds managed to sort of make the union work for a few months following Noni's birth. Then their father abandoned the family to pursue a country-music career. Oh, Humboldt Hoyt had promised to send for his wife and daughters once he 'made it.' Except, he never made it.

It pained Tania more than she could express that

her vagabond father hadn't RSVP'd his wedding invitation. On top of everything else, including a potential unplanned pregnancy and the omen of the destroyed shoes, how was she supposed to handle a disaster like the old church burning? She could barely see beyond *her* needs to consider what the loss of the structure would cost the congregation and the city.

"If there's no church," she asked, glancing at Trey, "how can we get married?" The logistics alone were staggering. Two morning ceremonies were on the docket at Rosewood Community Church, as well as two afternoon weddings. She had selected the last time slot, considering it the most romantic. No one would dare step a foot inside the historic structure following *their* ceremony. She hadn't meant forevermore! "What are the other couples doing?"

Trey shook his head. "I imagine they're in a mad scramble like we are."

"Or they're canceling," she whispered. "Rescheduling." The full implications of the fire burrowed into her jumbled thoughts. She was barely holding it together. "This is awful, honey. That beautiful church! The poor members of the congregation waking up to hear this dreadful news. What about the weddings and baptisms booked for later this summer and fall? What happens to the soup kitchen? People rely on Rosewood Community Church. What will they do?"

Concern filled his hazel eyes. "I don't know. But we live in a caring community, babe. The town and the church leadership will figure it out. Charities will step forward. You and I will donate a sizeable sum."

"As will I," Mom vowed from beside Tania's sisters. "I'll also volunteer to chair a fundraising committee. Whatever RCC needs."

A sad smile formed on Trey's mouth. His gaze turned to Tania. "As for you and me...and everyone else who planned on getting married in the old church today..."

"Oh, my God," she wheezed. Her instincts had proven eerily accurate. She and Trey *weren't* getting married. Not today.

Or ever?

She gasped as if breathing through a straw, yet her groom retained his legendary composure, pulling her against his chest again. Didn't anything discourage this man she loved? After four years, she should know everything about him. His level-headedness continued to surprise her. What would finally make him crack?

Tania burrowed her nose into the soft fabric of his *Last Chance for Bromance* shirt. Queasy sensations roller-coasted in her tummy as she took in the trace scents of hamburgers and French fries, which he must have chowed down during his round of golf with the groomsmen yesterday. Looking up at everyone, she touched her dressing gown sash. "Oh, Trey. First, my dad—" Her fingers twitched. "We don't even know if he's coming."

Tami's upper lip curled. "He's not coming."

Noni stood as silent as a garden gnome.

Tania let out a sob, and Trey kissed her temple. Eyes closed, she sensed her mom and sisters stepping closer, surrounding them. Love and caring emanated from her fiancé's sturdy chest, and from the presence of her family.

Mom's voice came softly from her left. "Tania, the news about the church is devastating, and we will deal with it, but please don't spare one speck of concern for your father's insensitivity. We don't need any man to pull off a wedding, sweetheart. Well, except for Trey."

"But—"

"Shush, darling. There, there." Mom rubbed her upper back. "I've told you repeatedly, you can't trust a man who wanted your middle name to be *Tucker-*

belle, for heaven's sake. I'm lucky I got away with Denise." The middle name of the iconic country star, Tanya Tucker. Dad had named each daughter after a Nashville music legend. Much to his displeasure, Mom altered the spellings.

Glancing at her mom from the warmth of Trey's embrace, Tania pressed a knuckle into an itchy corner of one eye. "If you couldn't trust Dad, then why did you marry him?"

Mom's palms opened. "I thought I was *in love*." Mom spoke the words as if her former affection for their father was an affliction. "He held this strange power over me. Like one of those sparkly vampires in the books you girls devoured as teenagers. It's a sad excuse, and our marriage was a poor example of a healthy relationship, but I was smitten." She patted Tania's shoulder. "It wasn't meant to be, but he gave me *you*, sweetie. He gave me Tami and Noni. My little sticks of TNT." Mom murmured the childhood group nickname for Tania and her sisters.

Trey cradled Tania's cheek against his shoulder. "My T-*L*-T," he whispered into her ear, and her heart melted. His acronym stood for a private endearment. She was his *True Love, Tania*. And he was her *True Love, Trey*.

She longed to stay in his embrace forever. To

luxuriate in the love blossoming in her chest. Because of his steadiness. His unwavering presence.

But panic pounced, quick as a cougar. She had planned a flawless wedding. Every detail. Every aspect.

"A perfect beginning leads to a perfect life," she whispered against Trey's shirt. Her face heated at her ridiculousness. He—and the cluster of cells possibly making itself at home within her uterus—deserved better.

She was a woman of science. A teacher. A member of an honored profession intended to nurture and help develop young minds. Despite two bachelor's degrees, somehow she'd allowed the overabundance of wedding myths perpetuated on TV and the internet to suck her into a woolly-feeling wormhole.

"Tania," her mom said. "Let's focus on the issue at hand."

"Which issue is that?" Tania stared at her family. Did Mom think some magical wedding fairy would appear with a glittery wand, a twinkle in her eyes, a skip in her step, perhaps even a crystal-embossed pumpkin coach, and fix everything? "Someone has to say it. Everything is going wrong." Throat clogging, she looked at Trey. "Maybe our wedding isn't meant to happen. Maybe we need to stop fighting the inevitable and accept that."

"We *are* getting married," he said in a firm voice. "It's time to bring in reinforcements, that's all." He exchanged a look with her mom.

Mom nodded. "My handsome son-in-law is spot on."

But Trey *wasn't* Mom's son-in-law. Not yet.

Tami's eyebrows lifted. "What sort of reinforcements?"

"Our friends," Trey said at the same time Mom declared, "Their friends."

Trey swung an arm like a high school football coach. "Let's get the group together, put on our thinking caps, and do this thing."

Noni cheered. "Do the damn thing."

A frown pulled on Tania's lips. "Our wedding is not a *thing*."

"Hey." Trey trailed his thumb across her cheek. "The woman I proposed to takes bad news on the chin and moves forward." His gaze locked on hers, and they stepped away from her family. In a quiet voice, he added, "The woman who stood by me when my dad and uncles were fighting lets nothing get her down."

"Not even multiple calamities occurring within

minutes?" she whispered, gliding a hand over her woozy tummy. "How many catastrophes are we supposed to take on the chin, honey?"

"As many as the day requires." He tucked a stray lock of her long hair behind her ear. "Tania. Love. Will we let this news change our plans? Or work together to achieve our dreams?"

"Work together," she whispered, the carsick sensations in her stomach swimming upstream. *Oh, no. Keep it down, Tania. Keep it down.*

But whatever—or whomever—had seized control of her body paid zero attention.

She doubled over at the waist and tossed the crumbs of yesterday's spa cookies onto Trey's shoes.

Chapter Three

T REY NEEDED to get to the bottom of his bride's curious behavior. They sat at the breakfast table in her mom's kitchen, phones at the ready and to-do lists fanned out in front of them. To look at Tania now, in the chair to his right, sounding composed as she spoke to the minister on her mom's extra work phone, he wouldn't guess that an hour ago, out in the driveway, learning about the church fire had made her physically ill. Concern rippled through him. Was she coming down with something? Or was her queasiness stress-related? It wouldn't be the first time she suffered tummy issues under pressure. Hopefully, solving the problem of where to hold their wedding ceremony would help her feel better.

Studying a tablet for alternate venues for this

afternoon, he listened to her side of the call. His optimism mounted as she smiled and nodded at something the minister said. While he couldn't shake the feeling that she was hiding something, he reminded himself the most tranquil woman would panic upon learning the church had sizzled into charred rubble. Might even consider the fire a doomsday sign of unrest down the line.

Tania's sensitive stomach aside, in the seconds before she'd upchucked little more than bile, her skin had taken on a greenish tinge. *That* was something Trey hadn't witnessed in his life.

After helping her inside the house, he'd poured her a glass of water and rustled up a box of crackers. He'd cleaned his shoes out of sight in the utility room in case the unpleasant aroma stirred another bout of nausea. He'd offered to accompany her upstairs while she showered and changed into her current skirt and top. Gaze anxious, she'd insisted on managing on her own.

Then Noni, expressing guilt about the ruined sandals, followed Trey's fiancée to the second floor despite Tania's protests. Noni had trailed her older sister around the house like a scolded puppy ever since.

Even now, Noni hovered, shoulders hunched

up around her ears as her fingers flew on her phone. Would it help if he assigned her a concrete task?

He beckoned over the younger woman. "Heath should arrive soon with the tuxedoes," he informed Noni in a hushed voice. "Would you mind waiting outside and showing him that parking spot along the side of the house?"

Releasing a weary sigh, she nodded. "Sure thing. Thank you, Trey." She scuttled toward the entryway.

Tania shot him a grateful look. After another moment, she said goodbye to the minister and disconnected.

Trey set aside the tablet borrowed from her mom. He interlaced their fingers on the tabletop. Tania gazed at him a bit awkwardly.

"Thank you for finding something for Noni to do," she murmured, casting a glance in the direction her sister had headed. "She's like my shadow. I can't get a minute alone."

"Try not to worry about it. She feels bad about your shoes."

"I know, but this is *our* day." Tania wriggled on her chair. "And I have news."

Piecing together portions of the phone call, Trey guessed, "Esther"—the minister at Rosewood

Community Church—"can still perform our ceremony?"

Tania's mouth curved in a half-smile. "At four o'clock, like we planned." She paused. Her left ring finger, devoid of her engagement diamonds for the ceremony, trembled. "Esther sounds overwhelmed but says she's happy to marry every couple who can find another venue within a reasonable driving distance. That includes you and me."

Trey restrained himself from dashing into the living room and jumping on the couch. "You bet it does," he said in a low voice, squeezing his bride's fingers.

Tania's even front teeth sunk into her plump lower lip. "One couple is postponing."

"Not us," he stated. He angled his head. "Unless you really want to." Whether to delay their plans wasn't solely his decision to make.

She drew in a breath. "Not us." Her smile sweetened, reaching her fair-lashed eyes. "Esther is emailing names and phone numbers of officiants who can take over a ceremony last-minute, depending on where each couple lands."

"That's incredible." Emotion thickened Trey's throat. "Good work, Love."

She blushed. Her shoulders lifted. "It wasn't

only me. The other bride and one of the double grooms have been in touch with Esther too."

"But *you're* incredible. And you're my love."

A pretty glimmer lit her eyes. "Aw. I love you, Trey," she whispered, head tilting at an irresistible slant.

"I love you," he murmured, leaning over to place a tender kiss on her soft lips. Desire thrummed in his veins as she let out the sensuous sigh he hadn't expected to enjoy again until they were husband and wife. He didn't care if a friend wandered in from the rec room and caught them in a moment of mutual adoration. Tania could turn him inside-out with one flirtatious look, and he was way more than okay with that. Gliding a palm along her shoulders, he broke the kiss and skimmed a finger along the sexy hollow between her bottom lip and the silky curve of her chin.

Her shoulders gave a sensuous shimmy as goosebumps dotted her neck. He would kiss those goosebumps into submission later tonight once they were married and alone. His excitement grew.

"Back to our lists," she said in a husky voice, gaze dipping. "How are your parents making out with contacting local guests about the fire?" She picked up a pen. "Should we ask someone to lend them a hand?" She positioned the pen above a list.

Trey rested a palm on the table. "Unnecessary. Our Puget Sound friends and family have been notified."

"Already?" Tania blinked. "That's fantastic." She crossed off an item written in his messy scrawl.

"Yep," he confirmed. "My cousins and an aunt helped. Any Seattle friends and relatives who haven't been assigned a job for today are waiting to hear where we're moving the ceremony. The hotel notified the out-of-town guests of an impending change."

Tania's forehead furrowed. "But Saturday afternoon traffic is crazy, Trey. What if we can't nail down a new venue close to the ballroom?"

Not wanting to inundate her with unnecessary information, he chose his next words carefully. "The caterers and the DJ will move the reception, if it comes to that." He hoped to hell it wouldn't. After the chaotic summer, the fewer complications dumped onto his bride's lap this morning, the better.

Her gaze widened. "Really? That's amazing."

"Your mom called the caterers while you and Noni were upstairs. The DJ texted me and offered to move to a new location. Such generosity. It blows me away."

Tania set down her pen and splayed a palm on her upper chest. "We're so lucky."

He smiled. "The reps said it was the least they could do. I made it clear we'll pay any additional costs. The caterers and the music dude shouldn't have to take a financial hit because of the fire." As well as rearranging those two enormous pieces of their day, at Trey's request, his younger brother Heath had put out feelers to a social-media group of western Washington farmers about possibly moving the reception *and* the ceremony to a rural location. If the stars lined up, Trey's brother would arrive at the house with not only the tuxedoes but venue options in hand.

Trey didn't want to reveal specifics too early, getting up Tania's hopes only to have them crash and burn.

"We just need to find a place large enough to accommodate everyone," he noted. In the two years since he'd proposed to the love of his life, their wedding had snowballed to include five brides-maids and just as many groomsmen, a flower girl and ring bearer, and one-hundred-sixty-four guests. And he wasn't quite sure how it had happened.

He couldn't feign complete innocence. Aided by one of their bridesmaids, he had a surprise in store for Tania as she walked down whatever last-minute aisle their families scraped together. He hoped the arrangement worked out.

"Just?" Tania echoed, her copper-penny-colored eyebrows bunching. "Trey, moving the ceremony—never mind the reception—is a lot." Gnawing her lip, she smoothed her fingertips over a to-do list. "I hate to bring this up, but should we ask guests outside of our immediate families *not* to attend the ceremony?" Shadows flitted in her gaze. "I mean, everyone can attend the reception. The ballroom is booked. And standing."

"Tania..."

"Hear me out. If we trim the ceremony numbers, we wouldn't need to worry about a change in officiants or people driving all over Greater Seattle. Esther from Rosewood Community Church could marry us in Mom's backyard." She gestured toward the hall leading to the rec room. From there, glass doors opened to a lush green lawn and beautiful flowerbeds.

Trey shook his head. "I don't want any of our guests feeling left out." If their wedding hadn't ballooned into a hot-air ride coasting across the

Rosewood skies, he might reconsider. But several family members and friends had traveled from out of state, and a groomsman had flown in from another country. Local friends and families had carved a day out of their weekends to help him and Tania celebrate. Cupping his bride's chin, he brushed her cheek and whispered, "More importantly, my TLT, I want today to be as close to perfect as possible. To be everything you've dreamed about." He ran his other hand through her silky hair.

Her gaze softened. "As long as we're married before the day is over, that's all I need." She leaned in for another kiss, which he accepted without hesitation. His body stirred as he swept wispy tendrils of hair off her forehead. "Something's bothering you," he whispered. "I can tell." And it wasn't the destruction of the church.

"I'm fine," she responded in a scratchy voice. "I was feeling off earlier. Nerves. I think."

He placed a palm on her forehead but didn't detect a fever. "How do you feel now?"

"Better." She wobbled a hand. "The queasiness comes and goes."

"Do you need to lie down?"

"Honey, I'm okay. If something were seriously wrong, I would tell you." Her gaze skittered away, and a lump lodged in his throat. A heartbeat later, she looked at him again. His uneasiness settled as she explained, "At some point, considering I didn't expect to see you until four o'clock, I'll need time alone." She paused. "To freshen up."

He nodded. "To get into your wedding gown and enjoy your mom and sisters and bridesmaids making a fuss. Of course." The specifics of where the dressing of the bride would now occur remained to be seen.

She wet her lips. "Also, to make sure we don't receive more surprises."

"We can handle surprises."

A shy smile touched her mouth. "When you look at me like this, I believe it," she whispered.

"Good," he whispered back, running his hand along her shoulder again and kissing her. He and Tania loved each other. That, he knew. Sometimes, remnants of insecurities from her childhood spilled into their relationship. Now and then, she expressed doubts about not feeling good enough for him—or for anyone, for that matter—to stick with her through thick and thin. As the oldest of the three Hoyt daughters, their father's plans for a nebulous future and his eventual abandonment had hit Tania the hardest. She and Trey discussed those upsetting feelings whenever they bubbled to the surface. Was she revisiting old hurts now?

Her gaze lowered to her lap. Heart thumping, Trey glued his butt to his chair and reeled in the urge to press for answers she might not wish to discuss on their wedding day.

When at last she looked up, her smile tilted at a peculiar angle. "You and I can handle anything life throws at us. Right?"

He chucked the soft skin beneath her chin. "You know it."

"That includes more bolts from the blue that, say, might occur between now and when we say, 'I do'?"

"The church went up in a puff of smoke," he noted dryly. "What could top that?"

She caught the edge of her bottom lip between her teeth. "Maybe something could go right...at the wrong time?"

He narrowed his gaze. "What are you trying to say?"

She shook her head. "Nothing."

He slid a hand beneath her hair, kneading her nape. "Tania. What is it?"

Her gaze caught on a movement behind his chair. "Later," she whispered as a genuinely joyful smile broke over her face. She got up and turned. "It's not bad," she whispered over her shoulder. "But something I need to confirm."

He stood. "Regarding?"

Sliding her palms over her skirt, she chirped, "Look. Janie and Keon are here."

Glancing toward the hall, Trey spotted his long-time friends, Keon Rivers and Janie McAllister, entering the kitchen. Keon, a groomsman, arrived from Canada last Sunday. Janie was one of Tania's closest friends and a bridesmaid. Keon and Janie had dated toward the end of Keon's research year with Whitaker Organic Farms. Keon returned to British Columbia a little over twelve months ago. Upon his arrival in Rosewood for the wedding, he and Janie had experienced a false start or two but ultimately picked up where they'd left off, discovering they were 'meant to be,' as Tania would say.

Two nights ago, Keon proposed, and Janie said yes.

Now, the couple radiated bliss as they swept into the kitchen. An engagement ring sparkled on Janie's left hand.

Trey beamed. "Hey, you guys."

Tania gushed, "Janie, show me your ring."

Janie spread her fingers and stepped toward Tania. The women squealed and chatted.

Trey shook Keon's hand. "Congratulations," he said to his old friend. "We were excited beyond words to hear the news." While Keon and Janie had put forth a valiant attempt to keep the change in their relationship status under wraps during last night's rehearsal dinner at a popular restaurant, the couple's obvious happiness prompted questions from mutual friends, and the news leaked. With Tania's encouragement, Keon and Janie had announced their engagement over dinner.

Keon grinned. "Thanks. I hope we didn't steal your thunder."

"Are you kidding me? After the church incident, your news is exactly what we needed for a boost, to carry us through these last-minute difficulties."

"Yeah. Unreal about the fire, eh?" Keon slapped Trey's shoulder. "Don't worry one whit, Whitaker. We'll get you hitched."

Trey chuckled.

"Honey," Tania called, swinging Janie's hand as the women strolled toward himself and Keon. "If you and I manage to get married today, it looks like these two are next."

Janie and Keon exchanged a besotted look.

"Go on." Tania nudged Janie. "Spill."

Janie's cheeks turned pink. "We're thinking about holding the wedding a year from September. In BC."

Tania clapped. "I love the idea! A destination wedding."

"A little over a one-hour plane ride away," Janie added.

"We're in," Trey said, hugging Janie.

Tania's gaze dropped to her fingers, and she began counting. Her thumb popped up. Then her index finger.

"What are you figuring out?" Janie asked with a smile.

Tania gulped. "Um, the hours until I'm chained to this man for life?" She secured her elbow through his.

The foursome laughed, and Trey's grin nearly split his face. Over the last couple of weeks, every woman in his fiancée's close circle of girlfriends had paired up with an upstanding guy. Now that *he* was nearly off the market, he supposed they'd needed to set their sights elsewhere. He allowed himself a quiet chuckle.

"What's funny?" Tania asked, poking his ribs as

Keon and Janie walked ahead of them toward the rec room.

He snuggled her neck. "Just patting myself on the back."

"Uh-huh. I know. I know. You set the bar." Short of the rec room, she swiveled within his embrace. "Everyone's lives are changing," she whispered, kissing him.

"For the better."

"Agreed." She drew in a breath, her gaze traveling over his face. "You know what? Change is good. Change is okay."

"Okay?" he pressed. "Or good?" He voted for the latter.

"That depends on the change," she whispered with a secretive lowering of her eyelashes.

"Hmm. Does this change have anything to do about more possible bolts from the blue?"

"Maybe."

"A woman of mystery? I love it." He kissed her cheek. *He* had a surprise for her at the altar, and it appeared she'd come up with a way to make the day extra-special for him as well.

Noise and excited conversation erupted from the rec room. "Oh, no," Tania said, releasing his hand and entering the big room ahead of him. "I hope it isn't Mr. Sprinkles again." She bent at the waist, her palms on the fronts of her thighs and her gaze swinging left and right as she scouted the base of the wet bar for the beginning-to-become-a pain-in-his-ass cat.

Trey spotted his groomsmen and childhood friends, Freddy and Eddie Pike, plus his college buddy, Ren Tomasko, also a groomsman. The guys stood grouped with Tania's bridesmaids and other friends near the glass sliders to her mom's gardens. Trey's younger brother emerged from the crowd. Heath lugged a heaping armload of tuxedo bags toward a nearby garment rack. He must have entered the house from the gate in the fenced side yard.

Heath held the garment bags while Keon hung them one at a time on the rack. Trey pushed two suits to the far end to make space for the rest.

"Did you see Noni?" he asked Heath.

"Yeah," his brother responded, passing Keon a suit bag. "She showed me where to park, then went to help Bea and Tami. Something about wedding flowers. They'll be here in a minute." Heath leaned toward Keon, who relieved him of another bag. "You won't believe who the Pike boys saw climbing out of a limo," Heath whispered dramatically. *"Boldt Tapper."* His gaze widened.

"Boldt?" Trey's jaw clamped closed. *Great. Sucky sense of timing, buster.*

He shot a glance toward Tania, who stood behind the wet bar, scrutinizing a selection of beverages in a tub of crushed ice. The presence of her mom's cat evidently no longer an issue, she traipsed her fingertips along a bottle. Trey headed her direction.

"Boldt who?" Keon asked Heath as Trey walked past his friend and his brother. "The *Great Gams* guy?" Keon whispered.

Heath nodded. "Yeah," he said in a quiet voice. "I recognized the dude's name, but what the hell are gams?"

"Slang for a woman's legs," Keon replied, hanging the last tuxedo bag. "The phrase is all over the classic detective novels your brother's brain eats like candy. Ever hear that kitschy song from the '90s, *She's Got Great Gams?*"

"It's about Bea," Trey muttered as Tania meandered out from behind the wet bar, a beverage bottle in hand.

"Dude knows Tania's mom?" Heath rasped.

"Dude's stage name isn't something the family

runs around sharing, but yes," Trey said. He hoofed it toward Tania as a tall man in his mid-fifties with long brown locks, striking blue eyes, wearing faded jeans, boots, a black cowboy hat, and carrying an acoustic guitar on a leather strap, sauntered through the parting crowd on the opposite end of the room.

As fate would have it, Tania's mom and sisters entered from the hall. The sisters' heads tipped together as they chattered about bouquets and boutonnieres.

Reaching his fiancée, Trey slipped an arm around her shoulders. "Honey—"

But the damage was done. Tania's gaze winged to her wandering-minstrel father. *"Dad?"* The beverage bottle dropped, landing on a rug and rolling beneath the cabinets. "You came?"

Her sisters gasped.

Bea's green eyes slitted. *"Humby!* How *could* you?"

A hush fell over the crowd.

Humboldt Hoyt, famous throughout the country-music scene as one-hit wonder, Boldt Tapper, strummed an unfamiliar tune on his guitar and strutted toward Tania and Trey.

"When I see my little girl," Tapper sang in his deep bass voice, his achy-breaky swagger on full display.

"So dressed up and so pretty..." The musician paused, winking at Tania, who froze in place.

Trey tightened his arm around her shoulders, offering his love and support without talking over her or otherwise speaking on her behalf. "You've got this," he whispered against her ear.

"I do," she returned in an unsteady voice. "But—"

"Sorry for the inconvenience, darlin'," Tapper interrupted. "I wanted to surprise you at the church once you were wearing your wedding gown and veil." The man strummed another chord. "After hearing the bad news, I told my driver, *'You know what?'*" Tapper sang his question in the same unfamiliar melody as his song. "A good daddy would come straight to the house."

Tania's face screwed into a knot of hurt. "A *good* daddy?"

"One second, Tanny," Tapper said, facing the shocked-into-silence assembly. His back to his daughters and a thunderstruck but clearly fuming Bea, the musician drawled in a grandiose manner, "My new song, *It's a Pity*, is droppin' durin' the weddin.' I wrote this song 'specially for my Tanny-Tee-Tee." Tapper smiled back at Tania and her sisters before singing to their slack-jawed friends,

"When I see my little girl...So dressed up and so pretty...It just makes me wanna be...The man I can't. It's a pity." Spinning on his cowboy boots, the musician strolled toward Bea. His fingers plucked guitar strings.

Red washed Bea's angry features. Tania's sisters remained shellshocked, eyes wide and jaws dropped.

Tania gaped as the musician's voice lowered further. *"Woe, woe, woe,"* he sang to Bea. Then he smiled. "Hello, Bea-Bunny. Happy to see your ol' Humby?"

Trey's fuming, soon-to-be mother-in-law reached back her hand and soundly slapped the country star's face.

Chapter Four

For Tania, the next few moments passed in a slow-motion blur. Her heart felt as if it had plummeted from its lifelong position inside her ribcage, sunk past her stomach, and flopped onto her open-toed sandals, not unlike a dying fish.

All her constant striving for a flawless wedding, a stylish apartment, and babies arriving at pre-planned intervals starting two years after her fiancé's yet-to-open business found its feet—everything she had mapped out for her future since her late teens to prevent her life from going off the rails —was unraveling.

She couldn't even control the events unfolding on *this* milestone day, intended to set the tone for their marriage.

Trey's powerful arm remained around her shoulders. He squeezed tight. "I can't believe the gall of this guy," he mumbled against her hair.

"He's my father," she whispered, placing a palm on the *Last Chance* lettering of his golf shirt. His heartbeat pounded beneath the pad of her thumb. His muscles coiled. "Hold steady, honey," she whispered. Her father hadn't been blessed with the sense of a chipmunk, but the little girl inside her craved his approval regardless. She murmured, "This is my dilemma. And my mom's. We'll take the lead." She knew without asking that Trey wanted to stand up for her and help fight her battles, because that was his nature. He was honorable, caring, and supportive. A hundred times the man her father had proven to be throughout her twenty-seven years.

Trey understood from a simple gesture when she needed him to stand aside and let her prove she'd inherited the dynamo gene from her diligent mother. Now that she realized pregnancy hormones might be responsible for some of the wimp factor ruling her emotions, she felt more than ready to step up. The tiny life potentially growing inside of her provided additional incentive.

Trey released a breath and nodded. Ten granite-faced groomsmen and bridesmaids, along with eight or so of their friends, mumbled amongst each other. Tania's sisters stared at Dad. As Dad's guitar swung on its embossed-leather strap, banging his spine, he traced the red imprint of Mom's slap against his whiskered cheek.

His boots clomped on the tiles. "Hot damn, Bea. What was that for? Settle down."

"*Settle down?*" Mom held a palm toward Tania, her narrowed gaze conveying her need to handle this insult. She glared at Dad. "Humboldt Hoyt, when in the history of humankind has anything remotely positive arisen from a man instructing a woman he has done wrong to *settle down*?" If Mom possessed the ability to sprout devil horns on command, they would have jutted from the top of her auburn bob at that moment. "And what the hell do you mean by what the hell was that *for*?"

Dad flinched, his whiskered chin disappearing into his gray plaid shirt.

Mom accused, "You have some nerve strolling into my house when our daughter and her fiancé— whom you have yet to meet, I might add—her sisters, her friends, and I are trying to salvage their wedding."

Dad's palms spread. "I'm here now."

Tania crossed her arms over her blouse. Moving

into lockstep position beside her mom, she frowned. "Why *now*, Dad? We mailed your invitation to your Nashville address. After the deadline came and went, Mom emailed your website *and* your team. Noni texted the last phone number any of us knew existed. Tami messaged your social media profiles. You didn't say squat."

He wrestled with the guitar bumping his left elbow. The strap tangled in his grasp. "Could someone help me out here?"

Their friends and family stood as still as headstones. Except for Noni. Her face crumpled, and a tiny sob escaped her mouth.

A scowling Tami indicated their youngest sibling. "Daddy, look what you've done now." Tami walked Noni to an easy chair. Tania's heart softened at the show of sisterly support.

"Now, now," Dad said, hands lifting as if he were addressing a rowdy crowd—or was about to get arrested. Eyeing Trey, he set the guitar on the craft table where their friends had made new wedding decorations last weekend after Mr. Sprinkles destroyed the originals.

Tania glanced over her shoulder at Trey and nodded. He crossed his arms and moved to her left, placing her protectively between himself and Mom.

Heart swelling, Tania gave him a small smile. She had loved Trey Whitaker almost since the day they'd met, and she wanted to marry him. But she needed to come clean—to herself anyway—that until now part of her had wondered if they were destined to marry.

Throughout her childhood, before she and her sisters grew to appreciate the intricacies of adult relationships, their father had proclaimed his love for his daughters and their mother multiple times. In the end, however, Humboldt and Beatrice Hoyt weren't "meant to be." Dad had employed the same phrase in the sorry excuse for emails he sent his daughters some Christmases. Tania's mom had uttered the same philosophy in the driveway ninety minutes ago.

Over the course of Tania and Trey's engagement, Tania had wondered...what if she and Trey were fooling themselves? What if she failed as his wife? Or if he failed her?

Could they handle pressure-packed hard times? Or would their foundation crumble?

At twelve, she cind her best friend Claire vowed they wouldn't follow their biological parents' examples. Now, Tania might be carrying Trey's child. She didn't have more time to waste. She needed to summon her backbone.

She directed her gaze toward her father. "I am not," she enunciated, "your Tanny-Tee-Tee. I haven't been for years."

He slipped his hat off his head and grasped the brim. "I have good reason for not mailing back the wedding card."

Tania's eyebrows hiked. "The RSVP?" she clarified. "Which arrived at your last known address with a stamped return envelope, an email address, a phone number, and a request to use any or all three?"

"Uh." His Adam's apple bobbed. "Yeah. That."

Trey's gaze met hers. "I'd like to hear this," he said sardonically.

"Well," Dad mumbled toward his hat. "I've made mistakes. I'd like the chance to correct them." He looked up. "Starting today." He aimed a tentative smile toward Mom.

Mom harrumphed. "Your charm won't work this time, Hum*boldt*." Mom emphasized the second syllable of Dad's first name, now his stage name, which he, or a record label, or some manager or agent who might have considered themselves brilliant, or maybe hadn't known better, paired with the surname, Tapper.

Tania's father had literally named himself a tool. Boldt Tapper, indeed.

Dad waggled his eyebrows at Mom. "Sweet words worked well enough in the old days."

Mom snorted. "Ancient history. I'll say it now in front of witnesses." Mom waved a hand to encompass the group, whose members looked up and down the walls, out the glass doors, at the drinks in their hands, at each other. Gazes focused anywhere other than on Tania and her family. But their ears couldn't miss the none-too-quiet conversation. "I've put a lot of stock into appearances over the years," Mom said. "Since you ducked out on us, Humboldt. I plastered on a brave face, trying to show my friends and family and our daughters that I can manage— no, I can *thrive*—on my own."

"You've done a marvelous job with the girls—"

Mom's finger wagged. "I don't give a rat's rubber knuckles what you think about how I've raised our daughters. This is *my* family. You've hurt—you've hurt us too many times."

Dad's gaze swung to Tania. "Tanny," he pleaded. He glanced at Tami and Noni. "Baby girls?"

Noni's rear remained fastened to the cushion of

the easy chair, her spine tree-trunk-straight. Tami perched on a leather arm beside their little sister, legs crossed. Her fingers laced over her knee, and both sisters blinked like baby bats.

Tania stared at her dad. "By all means," she said, unable to keep the steel from her voice. "What's the reason you didn't RSVP?" As her world shrank to Trey, herself, and her family, she glimpsed Heath ushering the crowd toward the hall and kitchen, providing her family what little privacy her father's grand entrance permitted.

"I was overseas," he said as the last of their friends exited. "On tour." His finger swept toward his guitar on the craft table. "My fans in Europe and Asia are rabid for my music. I couldn't let them down."

Tania's chest pinched. "What about letting all of us down?" Would he never grow up?

His gaze wandered to a point above her head. "I needed to rearrange my schedule. After my manager and I settled some business matters, I realized it was too late to mail back the 'SVP." He spared a glance at Mom. "Bea might have objected if I emailed or texted my reasons at a later date." He looked at Tania. "Your mother is a stickler for rules."

Trey's chin jutted. "Don't blame Bea."

"I'm not." Dad's gaze traveled up and down Trey's frame. "You seem like a decent guy. You'll understand I decided to surprise Tanny by showing up at the church. To, well, you know…" One of his hands flopped. The other gripped his cowboy hat.

Expressionless, Trey said, "You'll need to fill in the blanks."

"First off, there's my song."

Mom sneered. "The pity song?"

"We've heard this part." Tania forced back a swallow, refusing to allow the stinging sensation burning beneath her eyelids to develop into mois-ture. Or, God forbid, full-fledged tears. "I get it, Dad. You planned to arrive at the church to coincide with your new song dropping. I'm a publicity stunt to you. Nothing more."

"Not a stunt." He anchored his boots on the floor in a wide-legged stance. "When the label decided to release *It's a Pity* close to your wedding, I couldn't help spotting the co-inky-dink of the dates." He actually said *co-inky-dink* instead of coincidence. "Yeah, my manager nudged up the timing a few days. Why not? *I'm* the dad." His free hand chopped the air. "*I* walk you down the aisle." Another chop. "My song drops." Chop-chop. "It climbs the charts." Chop. "We party at the reception. Everyone wins."

Tania gawked. "I don't win! My sisters don't win!"

"What an ass," Mom murmured as Tania restrained herself from pointing her father toward the nearest exit.

Trey stepped nose-to-nose with her dad. Cheekbones white and fists clenched, he said in a harsh voice, "Are you for real? If you weren't Tania's father, I'd kick your selfish butt into the street."

The sweep-a-woman-off-her-feet part of Tania swooned. Okay, so it wasn't the most appropriate time for her attraction to her nearly-husband to make itself known, but she welcomed the momentary distraction from her father's selfishness.

"Tania-love," Trey asked softly, without removing his gaze from Humbolt's. "Who do you want walking you down the aisle?"

"Mom," she replied without hesitation, loving him more than she thought possible at that moment.

"Hear that, Humboldt? Bea is walking *my* bride down the aisle."

Dad grimaced. "It's my parental right to attend the wedding. To share walking-down-the-aisle duties with her mother if need be."

Trey folded his arms over his chest. "Wow. You

don't quit, do you? For a guy who hasn't given two flips about his family for the past two decades, you're a *classless* act. It is *not* your right. It's a privilege."

Tears filmed Mom's eyes. Tania stepped behind Trey and reached a hand toward her proud mother.

Mom shook her head. "It's your day, honey," she whispered in a wobbly voice. "If you want your father to walk you down the aisle…"

Tania clasped Mom's hands. "I don't want that." The pain and hurt she'd carried since preschool thickened her throat. The child inside her who had longed to reconnect with her father for years, to establish some sort of relationship as an adult that might pave the way toward repairing emotional wounds in the future, remained. But she would not make a choice at her mother's expense.

Not today.

Not ever.

Mom inhaled. "If you want your dad and I to walk you down the aisle together…"

Tami and Noni rushed toward them. "What are you guys talking about?" Tami asked. "There's no aisle. The church burned."

"Mom, you're a wonderful mom," Noni chimed.

Tania and her sisters clustered around the

parent they counted on. Mom patted Tami's cheek. "We're only calling it an aisle, sweetie," she said. "Whether an actual aisle exists isn't the point."

Tami's chin lifted. She looked at Dad. "We don't need your help."

Noni went on, "You weren't the one who sat up with us or changed our puked-on sheets when we were sick. Sometimes I'd cry for you, but I didn't even know where you were. Mom was always there. So was Tania. And Trey is about to become our big brother."

"Our brother-in-law," Tami whispered behind a hand. "Otherwise, it sounds weird."

"Our brother-in-law," Noni repeated.

Tania hugged her sisters in a group with her mom. "I love you guys." She glanced at Trey. "And I love you," she whispered.

"Love you," he whispered back, stepping close and rubbing her shoulder, his eyes crinkling in a tender smile.

It seemed strange, but a wave of relief rolled through Tania. She thanked every star in the universe that her father *had* come to the house. In an ironic turn of events, the fire at Rosewood Community Church was a sort of blessing in disguise. Not for the minister or the congregation, but for herself and Trey. It would have been so much worse if Dad had arrived at the chapel strumming his guitar—*when?*

As she walked down the aisle on her mom's arm?

Or before that, in the vestibule, while her bridesmaids fussed with her veil?

In the bridal chamber even earlier?

Dad might consider a surprise wedding appearance a promotion opportunity boxed as a gift, but to Tania the idea of him arriving at the church in his guitar-strumming glory inspired images of trying to navigate her way out of a cornfield maze at Halloween—shock after shock after shock hitting her between the eyes. She couldn't imagine dealing with the fallout.

The sound of Dad clearing his throat reached her ears. "Ladies. Trey. I hate to break this up—"

Mom faced him. "You don't hate to do *anything* that advances your career. Such as it is."

"That remains to be seen," he returned. "For now, I would like to go on record—pardon the pun —as saying I am realizing the error of my ways." He coughed into a fist. "Girls," he continued in a rough voice. "I haven't been the best daddy, but I mean to make up for my misdeeds."

Trey scoffed. "A man atones for his mistakes with actions, not hollow words."

Tania gazed longingly at her fiancé. Right then, she fell triple in love with him. Trey hadn't uttered a meaningless word to her during the four years of their relationship. He meant what he said, and he did what he promised. Her knees weakened as she tumbled more and more in love with this man she trusted with her hopes and dreams, through hard times and challenges, for the remainder of her years on earth.

"I *will* make up for the past with my future actions," Dad declared. "I'll admit that maybe dropping the song during the wedding was a bit of a stunt. But I have friends in the Puget Sound. A music producer. A tech giant. Well, come to think of it, the producer knows the tech guy, not me, exactly. Tania, the point is, I can nail down a private, park-like setting for your wedding." He snapped his fingers. "Like that."

"If I were a witch," Mom muttered. "I could make you disappear." She snapped her fingers. "Like that."

One corner of Trey's mouth curved upward. "Go, Bea."

Mom's expression darkened. "Darn it." She

gazed at Tania. "That was uncalled-for. Sorry, sweetie."

"It's okay."

Mom looked at Dad again. "I retract my outburst." To Tania, she said in a warm voice, "It's your wedding day, sweetheart. If you want your father at the church—" Mom paused. "You know what I mean. Wherever we hold the ceremony." Her voice regained some of its customary bluntness. "Not strutting his stuff down the aisle, or the gravel path, or the grass patch. But if you want him seated on our family's side of the new place, *far* away from the Whitaker side, whether he plunks his rump into a pew or a plastic chair, preferably near the back, I will understand."

"Tanny, I can change," Dad petitioned, fingers creasing the brim of his cowboy hat. "Um, my clothes." He ran a hand down his plaid shirt. "I can change my clothes."

Tania's palm fluttered to her tummy. "I can't possibly decide something like this on the spot." Would her father become a grandparent in fewer than nine months? Any decision regarding his presence at her wedding wouldn't only impact herself and Trey. She might establish future expectations for interactions with their children.

Their *family*.

Mom stepped toward Tania and her fiancé. "I didn't mean to pressure you into deciding anything, dear," she said. "It's your choice. Maybe you and Trey can discuss things?"

"It is your choice," Trey murmured.

Tania burrowed into her fiancé's arms, savoring his warmth, his quiet strength and unending support.

"Can you talk to Dad for a second?" she asked Mom, sniffling. She needed to collect herself.

Nodding, Mom turned toward Dad. She crossed her arms. "Humby, if you intend to make amends to your daughters, you'll have to atone to all three of them. No picking and choosing. Also, I realize what I'm about to say will hurt you. Believe it or not, I don't take any pleasure in that." Mom hauled in a breath. "Unless Tania and Trey decide otherwise, you'll need to come up with some other way to reconnect with the girls. You will *not* use the release of your single to draw attention away from Tania and this fine young man on their wedding day."

Dad squinted sideways. "My amends can't begin today?"

From within Trey's embrace, Tania exchanged a glance with her sisters. Tami and Noni nodded, communicating without words that they would abide by her decision.

Tania gazed up at Trey. His eyebrows lifted. His head cocked.

Suddenly, her choice was crystal-clear.

Inching out of his arms, she walked toward her father. "I'll see if the videographer can set up a private livestream," she said in as gentle a tone as she could muster. "You can watch the ceremony from your hotel room."

Dad's chin pulled back. *"What?"* He glared at Mom. "This is your influence."

Noni gasped.

"Daddy!" Tami warned.

Heavy-heartedness enveloped Tania. She locked eyes with the man. "You pounded the last nail into your coffin, Boldt." She couldn't think of him as 'Dad' right now. Would she ever be able to again? "I can't risk you making a scene during the ceremony. Neither can I chance our guests or the few members of your extended family recognizing you at the reception. Or turning any portion of the day into a big, fat, Hoyt reunion spectacle." A rod of determination straightened her spine. "My wedding will not become social-media fodder." Clasping Trey's hand, she looked at Boldt. "You and I can talk when my husband and I return from honeymoon. No amends are happening today."

The entertainment facade that was Boldt Tapper crumbled for the space of a heartbeat, and a hint of a regular Joe emerged. The unfamiliar version of her father sighed. "I don't blame you, Tanny. I am responsible." Then a muscle in his cheek twitched. Boldt sprang back to life. The man's gaze landed on Mom. "And you wonder why a man won't stay."

"*Leave,*" Trey ordered. "Now." He pointed toward the glass door.

"Humby," Mom murmured in a tone as sweet as if the taste of honey lingered on her tongue, "fetch your guitar before I smash it." She smoothed her hair.

"You heard Mom," Noni said. "Before she crushes it rock-star style."

"Before every one of us takes a turn." Trey slashed out the words.

"This is ridiculous," Boldt growled. The tread of his boots echoing, he grabbed his instrument, plopped on his hat, yanked open the glass slider, and stomped into the backyard. "Text the livestream link," he barked before disappearing around the corner of the house, presumably to the side gate.

A slow breath seeped out of Tania. She looked at

Trey. "Thank you for letting me handle that, honey." She asked Tami, "Do you have his number?"

Her middle sister shook her head. "Do you have the number?" Tami asked Noni.

Noni's brow knotted. "Beats me. He hasn't responded to my messages in months. Maybe I've been texting a stranger." She looked at Mom. "Do you have it?"

Mom shrugged. "I could run out to the driveway and make sure we have the correct info before his limo peels away."

"No." Tania shook her head. "He can sweat it out for a few hours. I can't stand more drama this morning." Unless, of course, more stumbling blocks appeared while they located an alternate ceremony venue. Also, she needed to speak to Trey about the likely source of her queasiness. "Once we confirm wedding details, Heath or Claire can contact Boldt's manager through his website."

Trey smiled. He hugged her close. "I'm proud of you." He kissed her temple. "Your dad might surprise you and text someone for the livestream link before we need to go to all that trouble."

"That *would* be a surprise," Tania murmured.

But she could handle it. She could handle anything life threw at her. As long as she had Trey.

Chapter Five

"Okay, everyone," Trey announced to his soon-to-be family members, plus his and Tania's friends reassembled in a tight cluster in the rec room. "Listen up." He surveyed the group for Heath, but his brother hadn't returned. Hopefully, as the best man, Heath was busy arranging details for an alternate ceremony. "For those who didn't realize this until today," Trey continued, allowing his gaze to linger on each person a moment, "the country singer known as Boldt Tapper is Tania's father."

"And *our* father," Tami said, gesturing between herself and Noni.

"Also, my ex-husband," Bea added, rolling her eyes.

Trey exchanged a glance with Tania, who stood

to his left. A tremulous smile curved her mouth as she tucked a glossy strand of hair behind one ear. Before her sisters had let the group back in, she'd asked him to take the lead during this awkward post-Boldt-reveal information session. Now that he'd begun his speech, her complexion paled. Was she feeling crummy again? Or defeated?

He sidled his hand next to hers and slid his pinky finger along her thumb.

"It's cool," Freddy Pike, his gregarious buddy since the second grade, remarked. "Tania's dad is a celebrity."

"A minor celebrity," Bea mumbled, eyebrows arching.

Eddie, Freddy's brother and Trey's good friend since his and Heath's tree-fort days, nodded. "Boldt Tapper is considered D-list now, but when we were kids? Our dad loved his Great Gams song." Eddie jostled Fred. *"Hot damn,"* Eddie sang the opening lyrics to Boldt's greatest hit. *"But she's got great gams—"*

Freddy kicked up a foot. *"They're the only thing that keeps me comin' back, comin' back..."*

Eddie's elbows angled left and right. *"And the fire in her eyes..."*

"When she says it's Boldt she despises..." Freddy wriggled his hips.

Trey flung up his hands. "Hey! *No.* Guys, this is exactly the sort of behavior we don't want." He whispered to Tania, "Sorry." The Pike brothers were his rowdiest buddies but also good dudes. When he and Tania agreed to expand their bridal party to five per side to accommodate her sisters, Ed and Fred volunteered as extra groomsmen. "Pikes, everyone knows you like your fun, but you can entertain the guests with one of your *other* brother routines toward the end of the reception. For now, let's be clear: everything that occurred between Tania and her father this morning stays in *this* room." He pointed at the floor.

"Boldt isn't coming to the wedding," Tania said in a quiet voice.

"He won't be at the reception either," Trey stated, caressing her shoulder. Tania and her sisters had reached that conclusion without input from himself or Bea. Tania's sadness over the events rippled in her tone, which concerned him.

Would his bride and her father ever reconcile? Since Trey had popped the question, whenever they spoke about starting a family in a couple of years, she'd expressed a wish for her dad to become involved as a grandparent in some capacity. Could the issue be as simple as Humboldt honestly wanting to repair the wounds he had inflicted on his children, but the man lacked the emotional intelligence for how to go about it? Could Trey steer the fellow in the right direction?

He drew in a breath. That was a discussion for another day.

Or another year.

Bea scanned the crowd. "We're asking all of you, as Tania and Trey's closest and oldest friends, not to say a word about my ex-husband coming to the house or being in town. This matter needs to be kept under wraps until *at least* following the reception. Discuss the issue amongst yourselves for the next few minutes if you must. Once we have a location locked down for the ceremony, I want my daughter and son-in-law focused on *their* happiness. Nothing else."

Noni nodded. "We don't want our sister or Trey worrying about Dad or wondering what he might do."

"Word might get out that he's in town anyway," Tami tacked on. "In fact, he might make sure it does."

"Which is why he doesn't need anyone's help," Noni summarized.

Trey smiled at the two younger Hoyt sisters, then returned his attention to the group. "We've devised a solution that includes *no one here* posting to social media at any point throughout the day."

Ren Tomasko, another of Trey's friends and a groomsman, looked at Tania. "I would like to believe I speak for all of us when I say we would never risk adding more stress to a troubling situation." He glanced at the others. Their friends nodded.

"That's easy to say now," Trey said. "But after a few glasses of wine? Rubber lips sink ships."

Tania's fingers laced at her waist. "Which is why we're asking everyone in the bridal party to hand over their phones to my mom until after the reception."

Eddie's eyebrows pulled together like thick caterpillars. "What if our dad needs us? He hurt his knee last week."

"Eddie," Trey advised, surveying the group. "Fred, and anyone else. Check in with everyone you need to now. Provide temporary passwords if you like. Bea will monitor your phones. If something urgent arises, of course she'll return a device to its owner."

Tania released a sigh. "Sorry, guys. I know some of you looked forward to sharing photos and videos in real time, but this afternoon is a test of sorts for my father. To see if he can live up to his promises. We're arranging a livestream he can watch from his hotel room. Or wherever he's staying. If by some twist of fate, he recognizes the ceremony location and crashes the wedding *or* the reception, my sisters and I will understand the sort of man we need to deal with—or kick out of our lives." Her green eyes misted as she crooked a finger toward Claire Merriweather, her best friend and maid of honor.

Claire beelined to Tania, and Trey's heart clenched as the duo discussed the livestream while other friends gathered around them.

More than anything, he'd wanted to build beautiful memories today that Tania could recall with pride. He couldn't imagine dealing with a parent who behaved like a toddler. Skating his hand along her shoulder, he massaged her nape. She angled him an appreciative glance.

"Can you call the videographer from the house phone and confirm the livestream?" she asked Claire. "The minute we know where we're going, we'll touch base with her."

Claire nodded. The two friends hugged. "Don't worry one bit," Claire said. "I've got this."

Eddie and Freddy clapped Trey on opposite shoulders before shaking his hand.

"Everything will work out," Janie McAllister reassured Tania with the optimism of a newly engaged woman.

"I hope so," Tania whispered, glancing at the floor.

"Aw, babe," Trey murmured. Was she ready for today? Was he pressuring her into proceeding with their plans during an awkward time? "We should talk," he whispered against her hair.

"I agree," she whispered back, slipping her hand into his. "Upstairs."

His stomach tightened. "All right." She sounded plenty serious.

They headed toward the hall but didn't advance more than two paces when Heath sprinted into the room. Hollering, Heath waved his phone. "We got it! We got Bonners' Blueberries & Bliss!"

Tania's eyes rounded. "For the ceremony?"

"And the reception! It's up to you two. We can move the whole thing." Heath grinned.

Tania squealed. Their friends clapped and hooted.

"I thought Bonners' wasn't opening until the third week of August," Tania said, her palm on her upper chest.

"The renovations on the warehouse finished early," Trey informed her with a smile. The decades-old family-run blueberry farm sat a thirty-five-minute drive from Rosewood. When he and Tania got engaged, the Bonners hadn't announced their plans to host weddings and other large events. Regardless, Tania's first choice had been the historic church. Trey, excited for the Bonner family, had kept tabs on their progress.

Tania wiped a hand across her forehead. "Renovations finished early?" she echoed. "That's practically unheard of."

"Someone is smiling down on us," he agreed.

She clasped his hands. "Let's move the whole damn thing. The ceremony and the reception."

His heart leaped at her enthusiasm. "Babe, are you sure?"

She nodded. "The distance is drivable, but the farm isn't close to the wedding hotel. If the farm has everything we need—"

"They do," Heath broke in, dancing a jig. "Chairs, tables, decorations. They have the whole shebang. They want to make today work for you guys."

Claire squirmed. "It's thrilling."

"And overwhelming," Tania whispered, glancing at Trey.

He leaned toward her. "Let's talk before we decide. In private."

Her gaze roamed over his face. "We don't need to. Not about this. Trey, I want to marry you. Today." Raising their joined hands like an announcer presenting a prizefighter, she proclaimed to their family and friends, "Let's get this boat moving in the right direction!"

The group erupted into a cacophony of conversations and laughter as Tania's mom shepherded the crowd out of the rec room. Bea assigned tasks, and joy erupted inside Trey. He and the love of his life were tying the knot today.

As they stepped into the hall, Tania tugged his hand, separating them from the people heading toward the kitchen and living room. "Honey, we need to hang back."

He glanced over his shoulder, noting the concern crinkling her forehead. "Shit. I was right. Too much is changing too fast. No pressure, my TLT. We can get hitched at City Hall after our honeymoon. People will understand."

A smile curved her lips. "I am more than ready to

marry you this afternoon, my sweet man. At four o'clock, like we planned. But..." Her gaze shifted toward the staircase leading to the second floor. "I need to pee."

Chuckling, he indicated the powder room a few feet back. "I'll wait."

She nibbled a thumbnail. "I need to use the upstairs bathroom. There's a test up there. In my makeup bag."

"A test?" What was she telling him?

"A stick," she whispered, positioning her gaze inches from his. Their noses bumped. "Trey, I need to urinate. *On* the stick."

His throat dried. "A stick test?" He swallowed. "The kind a person might buy from a drugstore?"

Biting her lower lip, she nodded.

Stars burst behind Trey's eyelids. "But how? When?"

"Bainbridge Island. June." Tania hoisted their joined hands beneath her chin. As his heart pounded like jungle drums, she whispered, "I can't marry you before we know, honey. I might be pregnant."

The blood drained from his face. "Oh. Crap."

Shivery tingles raced up Tania's spine. "Trey, stop pounding on the door," she instructed her fiancé, prowling outside the second-floor bathroom. He must have pressed his face against the panel. She could hear his heavy breathing, as if he were a wolf-shifter in a steamy romance novel desperate to claim his mate.

Her pulse raced. Now a trembly and decidedly sensuous shimmy unfurled in her veins, heating her through. She shook her head. What was *wrong* with her, becoming aroused at a time like this?

"You're driving my anxiety through the roof, honey." He was jetting her attraction to him halfway to Europe.

His knuckles rapped, the noise a little quieter. "Babe," he mumbled in his one-more-minute-in-bed-sweetie voice. "Let me in."

Dragging air into her lungs, she slung the hand towel onto the holder and checked her reflection. "In a second." She swiped strawberry-flavored gloss across her lips. The digital pregnancy test sat on the counter. The three-minute countdown to determine if they would become parents within thirty-four weeks or so had begun.

Trey had indulged her wish to conduct the test alone. Honestly, over their engagement, he'd catered to her every whim regarding the wedding arrangements and the furnishings for their new home. The spare bedroom in their new condo was intended as a guest room, not a nursery.

Not for two or three more years.

Moments ago, her fingers had trembled and her heart had pounded as she'd located a clean receptacle. She'd washed and dried the tiny cup before relieving herself. She hadn't wanted to mess around attempting to pee *on* the stick. Following the second paragraph of instructions, she had dipped the absorbent tip into her sample instead. A woman's first morning stream typically contained the highest concentration of pregnancy hormone, and she'd gone a few times today already. If she botched *this* test, there wasn't a backup. She'd checked after shoving her fiancé out the door.

She fluffed her hair and checked her reflection before letting him back in.

He dropped a kiss onto her lips. His beard tickled. "You taste amazing." He arrowed for the vanity.

"Don't touch the test," Tania whispered, lifting her hand as his gaze zeroed in on the wand. "We don't have time to buy another." Before tearing open the wrapper, she'd messaged Claire that they would arrive at Bonners' Blueberries & Bliss two or three hours before the ceremony, allowing her and Trey plenty of time to determine the test results and freak out.

He glanced at her sideways. "I wonder whose it is?"

She whacked his arm. "*Yours*, silly."

"No." He laughed. "The test."

"Oh. Ha-ha." Was first-trimester brain affecting her already? She checked the flashing hourglass on the device. She glanced at her phone timer. "Two more minutes," she whispered, although no one other than the pair of them remained in the house. Their crew had dispersed to complete wedding tasks. "I wondered the same thing earlier," she said, placing her hand on Trey's shoulder blade and skating her palm along the cotton of his golf shirt. "At first, I figured the test belonged to Tami or Noni. Then I remembered Mom used to store an unexpired test somewhere in the house, in case any of us had a scare. Spotting the box this morning caught me off-guard." Yup, possible pregnancy fog.

Trey nodded. "That sounds like something your mom would do." He leaned his butt against the countertop and scooped her into an embrace. His hands rested on her waist, sending a shiver through her skin. He touched his forehead to hers. Their breaths mingled. "We might become parents next spring," he whispered.

Happiness bubbled inside her. "It doesn't bother you that this afternoon might be a shotgun wedding?" She grazed her fingertips along his close-cropped beard.

He shook his head. "No one in their right mind these days believes in pressuring a couple to get hitched because the bride is pregnant. Tania, *we* are tying the knot today because we love each other. Regardless of what this test says."

She licked her lips. "But a child...in seven to eight months...isn't what we planned." Worry tightened her in its grip. "Trey, if I'm pregnant, I can't keep your beautiful wedding gift. There isn't room for a baby car seat in a roadster."

"So that's what was bothering you earlier," he said with a light laugh. "These things happen," he added, as his lips touched hers briefly.

"*That's* what worries me." Unplanned pregnancies had happened to her mom three times.

"We'll exchange the car for a crossover," he said, curling his fingers behind her neck, below her hair. "No matter what the test says, I love you, Tania." He snuggled her close.

She detected movement between their bodies.

Inside his pants. She looked down. "Oh, my God. Trey, are you hard?"

"At the idea that I might've slipped a baby into the woman I love, despite our best intentions not to let that happen?" He grinned. "Hell, yeah. My swimmers deserve gold medals."

She didn't bother pointing out that—if she were pregnant—the miracle of new life had more to do with her cycle and the details of their wedding distracting her from packing birth control that fateful weekend. Instead, as his mouth claimed hers, his cheerfully announced, "*Hell, yeah,*" reverberated in her mind.

Her nerves calmed, and her desire mounted.

Omigod, they were both crazy. Crazy in love. Was it only a few hours ago she had wondered if the universe was sending her a message *not* to marry this wonderful man?

The timer beeped on her phone.

"Ready to check the results?" Trey whispered in her ear, zipping delicious frissons along her neck.

Unable to speak, she nodded.

He slid an arm around her waist. Together, they turned.

Tania swept her gaze over the digital readout. "Pregnant," she squeaked. She glanced at the conception pane. "Implantation likely occurred over three weeks ago."

"Bainbridge Island for the win!" Trey pumped a fist.

Tania pressed two fingertips to her forehead. "I have to stop taking my pills." Studies showed her birth control method was ninety-nine percent effective, unless a woman skipped doses. One weekend of carelessness had reduced the effectiveness to ninety-one percent, a figure Tania's mother had mentioned to her and her sisters countless times.

"Don't worry, my TLT," Trey whispered. He wrapped his strong arms around her hips and picked her up. He spun them around the spacious bathroom. "The baby will be okay."

Emotion thickening her throat, she nodded. Logically, scientifically, and according to the most recent medical statistics, he was correct.

"Excellent," he murmured in a husky voice, gazing deep into her eyes. He carried her into the hall and then into her old bedroom, her legs wrapped around his waist. He kicked shut the door, sealing them within the secluded room.

Tania lowered her lips for a taste of her one true love. "You're happy?"

"Babe." He brushed her hair away from his face. "I promise we aren't your parents. We have the money. We have our new apartment. We have a wonderful relationship. We even have a dog. So what if we're lacking a white picket fence? That's life these days. We are more than ready to start a family now."

"I'll need to go on maternity leave," she whispered as he placed her lovingly on the sheets and pulled back the bedcovers.

"There's time for planning once we return from our honeymoon. For now, let's celebrate." He sank onto the bed. His hand ran up her leg, inching beneath her skirt. His fingers toyed with the flimsy waistband of her bikini panties, scattering quivers of ecstasy between her thighs.

"Trey." She sighed. "Are you going to make a dishonest woman out of me?"

Moaning, he kissed her neck. "It's been too long."

"It's been two and a half weeks," she reminded him softly. "Of not having intercourse." They'd indulged in other amorous activities.

He gazed at her. His big fingers stroked the silky fabric of her panties, and her hips wriggled. "Didn't I just say that?" he asked, sounding pleased with himself. "It's been way too long since I've been inside you."

Her need for him ribboned throughout her body. "I'll be scouting out maternity undies before too long." She had no clue about the current options or trends in pregnancy panties, but just in case. "You'd better feast your eyes on this pretty pair while you can." She kicked off her sandals and reached for his pants zipper.

"I'll feast on you with more than my eyes," Trey mumbled, his intentions clear as his gaze dipped to her rapidly dampening panties.

Dizzying desire swirled inside her as they undressed each other in a rush.

"What sort of couple consummates their wedding hours before the ceremony?" she asked, breathless.

"Probably more than are willing to admit." Scooting his big body down on the bed, he made himself comfortable between her parted legs and lifted her hips in his hands. He presented her most private parts to his mouth like a meal.

Anticipation spinning, Tania arched her spine. His tongue found her wetness as she reached down and wove her fingers in his hair.

She couldn't believe they were doing this while

their family and friends were heading to Bonners' Blueberries & Bliss to set up their wedding. But—

"*Yes*, honey," she whispered as Trey licked and sucked her most sensitive areas. His whiskers grazed her inner thighs. "That's so good. Oh, Trey. I love you." She gyrated as he spiraled her ever closer to the edge. *"Trey."*

His lips released her nub, and his tongue gave a final slurp. She clutched the sheets, elation bearing down as he slid up and balanced his weight on his forearms.

His fingers grazed either side of her face with such tenderness that she almost wept. The pulsing at her core intensified.

"Tania," he whispered, pushing the tip of his erection inside. He moaned, remaining still for a tortuous moment. Then his gaze found hers. "You feel incredible." He plunged deep.

Groaning, she brushed a flop of hair off his forehead. They kissed and moved in unison as her pulse raced. The spot where they were joined thrummed.

He slid his hands beneath her rear and angled his hips, pumping faster. Her neck curved on the pillow, and she rode the highs of her passion until her world exploded into dazzling rays of light. She called out his name.

"Tania, I love you." After another thrust, he groaned. Long and low, ending in a growl.

"I love you," she whispered, kissing his face as he curled her beneath his arm and rested the back of his hand on his forehead.

He gazed up at the ceiling for a few quiet seconds. "Don't worry." He grinned at her. "We'll consummate the legal marriage later tonight."

She giggled. She didn't doubt it. "We need showers." She patted his muscular chest.

He placed a loving kiss on her lips. "Let's take one together. Then we'll grab everything we need from here and from our old place, and head to Bonners'."

Her stomach rumbled. "I'm starving." She lowered a hand to her tummy.

"Okay, mommy-to-be. First, we'll shower. Then we'll raid Nana Bea's fridge. *Then* I'm shackling you to me for the rest of our lives."

"Omigod, you're literally calling my mom a granny." She giggled. "I wonder how she'll take the news."

"She might be shocked at first, but she'll get over it. And she can choose her own granny name. It'll be fun."

"It's gonna be amazing." Their wedding this

afternoon. Also, the years of being a married couple and becoming a family lay ahead. "I can't wait."

"Same here." He grabbed his pants off the floor and retrieved his phone.

She sat up with bedsheets pooled at her waist. "Did a notification ding? Who is it?" They'd promised to hand over their devices to her mom once they arrived at the venue.

"No, to the first question," Trey responded. "None of your beautiful business to the second." His eyebrows bobbed. "I need to confirm a surprise for later today."

"*Another* surprise?" He was too much. "What is it?"

"Tania." He winked at her as he strode naked toward the hall, phone in hand and butt muscles flexing. "Telling you defeats the purpose of a surprise." Hand on the doorknob, he turned and held up his phone. "Give me two minutes to deal with this. I'll meet you in the shower."

Smiling, she flopped backward onto the pillows and crossed her hands over her heart. The pit-a-pat echoed against her palms. *Oh, my God.* They were actually doing this. They were going to tie the knot. Next spring, they would become parents.

She was the luckiest woman alive.

Chapter Six

Heart pounding much too rapidly for his liking, Trey paced the groom's suite in the newly renovated wedding and events center at Bonners' Blueberries & Bliss. The muscles on either side of his spine knotted. "What's taking them so long?" He scraped a hand through his styled hair, messing the front. He couldn't care less.

Heath touched his shoulder. "Dude, chill. You look like you're gonna pass out." Ren, Fred, and Eddie chatted and joked in the background.

"Yeah?" Trey said to his brother. "Well, having yet another thing go wrong at this point in the day will do that to a guy." He darted a glance to the tuxedo-themed clock on the reclaimed-wood wall.

The countdown to the ceremony had started. He swallowed past a dry lump in his throat.

Heath accepted a glass of scotch from Fred. "Here. Drink this." He handed Trey the crystal tumbler.

"Thanks." Trey gulped a healthy swig of the twenty-year-old single-malt his fiancée had selected for his pre-ceremony time with his groomsmen. The smoky flavor of the top-shelf brand swept a welcome trail down his gullet. Swiping his knuckles across his mouth, he thumped the glass onto a narrow farm table. "If she's not here in ten minutes—"

Heath snorted. "Big bro, if your *dog* doesn't make it to the ceremony because of some screwy issue with the Yorkie whisperer that's beyond your control, Tania will understand."

Keon cupped a tumbler. "Your fiancée doesn't know what you're planning."

Ren sipped his drink. "How can Tania miss out on something she has no clue might occur?"

Trey snapped the sleeves of his tuxedo jacket. "Because...this morning I let it slip I had another surprise in store for her today."

Heath laughed. "Trey, man, why would you do that? It's just asking for trouble."

"She caught me in a vulnerable moment," Trey muttered. He wouldn't say another word about his time with his fiancée in her old bedroom.

Heath scrutinized him for what felt like an eternity but probably amounted to three heartbeats. "All right," Heath replied in a calm voice. "We can handle this. Tania gave me instructions, lest you freak out."

"Lest?" Eddie parroted. "That's some fancy language you got going on." He chuckled.

Heath sent a crooked smile to their childhood friend. "Can it, Pikester One." His gaze swung back to Trey. "You need to relax. What you do is slowly breathe in for five seconds"—Heath demonstrated, inhaling through his nostrils—"and then slowly breathe out for a second set of five." A stream of air released from Heath's mouth. "Rinse and repeat as needed."

Trey practiced the grounding technique Tania had tried to teach him last week. His chest remained pinched in an invisible vise grip.

He grabbed his scotch and quaffed another mouthful. His married buddies had warned him about the hectic nature of a wedding day. Despite their talk, he hadn't expected his vital organs to feel like they would blast out of his body and zoom into orbit.

Heath's eyebrows lifted. "Better?"

"A little." Trey put down his glass. "Thanks, brother."

Heath squeezed his shoulder. "That's why I'm here."

A knock sounded at the door. Keon called, "It's open."

Alicia Maxwell swept into the suite, looking graceful despite her neon-pink bridesmaid dress.

Heath hid his eyes. "Whoa! We can't see you, Alicia. It's bad luck."

She laughed. "That's a superstition for the bride and groom, goof. And I think the ship of bad luck has sailed. Tania and Trey saw each other this morning. Remember?"

Trey scratched his neck, willing his pulse to slow before he asked the woman, "Any news on Teacup?"

"Yes." Alicia's eyes brightened. "Both dogs have arrived with the Yorkie whisperer. By the way, what a stroke of luck she had room to board Teacup until after the honeymoon."

"She saved our hides," Trey acknowledged.

Fred laughed. "She saved Bea's *cat's* fluffy and furious hide."

"Oh, you guys." Alicia joined in the merriment as Trey's little brother and his oldest friends clustered around. "Anyway," she said, "the Yorkie whisperer—darn it, her name escapes me—offers profuse apologies for giving the dogs a potty break at a pet park with a creek running through the grounds. Thank God for backup outfits, right? The pooches and the human are dried and dressed. Your guests have gushed over how cute Teacup and Spats look in their outfits. The trainer has those dogs harnessed and leashed, and that woman is loaded with treats and a fancy reward clicker. The dogs are happy."

Heath plucked the shoulders of his tuxedo between his index fingers and thumbs. "Seems I did a great job of getting Teacup to her wedding-dog sessions."

Alicia rolled her eyes. "With my help," she noted.

Trey hugged his brother and then Alicia. "Thank you both. I can't tell you what everyone's hard work today means to me. And what it means to Tania." He asked Alicia, "How is my bride feeling? Nervous?" Or nauseated?

He couldn't bring up the tummy problems without raising suspicions. Apparently, morning sickness occurred at any time of day. Before he and Tania left her mom's house, Tania packed a tiny container of crackers into her bridal gear. If the queasiness returned, she'd promised to nibble a few mouthfuls out of sight of her attendants.

Alicia flicked a hand. "Oh, she's bouncing all over the bride's rooms. Nerves on a wedding day are natural. So I hear," she went on with a smile. Gesturing around the groom's suite, she spun in a circle. "How amazing is this place? Situating the bride's rooms and the groom's suite on opposite sides of the chapel was pure genius. Fireworks could go off in here, and Tania wouldn't hear a thing." Alicia clutched Trey's biceps. She stared him in the eyes. "Your bride looks gorgeous. You are one lucky man."

"Don't I know it." Love expanded in his chest. He wanted to climb the rafters of the converted blueberry warehouse and shout to their guests that he and Tania would become parents next spring. But they'd promised not to breathe a word about the pregnancy until a visit to her doctor confirmed the results. That wouldn't happen until after the honeymoon.

"You look handsome," Alicia said, her gaze drifting over his face. She wiggled her fingers toward his forehead. "Maybe fix your hair. The top looks mussed."

"Yes, ma'am. I wrecked it. I'm a ball of nerves myself."

"I don't doubt it. Okay, Tania thinks I'm in the bathrooms in the main annex. I need to get back before she realizes something is up." She looked around at the group of guys. "Five minutes!"

"Wait," Heath said as she headed for the door. "Is the livestream ready?"

Trey exhaled a gust of air. "Good question." Was this how jugglers felt? That a ball might crash to the floor any second?

"Sorry," Alicia said, whirling around. "I blanked on updating you about that. Yes, the videographer popped in to show Tania the connection to her dad's tablet. Mr. Hoyt—Humboldt—Boldt, whatever he's calling himself, is sitting in his hotel room staring at the screen. Looking, if I don't mind saying, like a prisoner waiting to hear his sentence over a video-conferencing app."

Keon shook his head. "It's too bad things had to turn out this way."

Alicia shrugged. "The man made poor choices. Now he has to live with them." She looked at Trey again. "Seriously. Your hair." She pointed toward the oval mirrors.

Trey laughed. "Okay, okay." She left, and he

headed to the mirrors. He fixed his hair and tided his beard while his brother and his groomsmen supervised.

"*Now* you look like a man who's about to get hitched," Heath said, passing Trey his scotch tumbler. A half-finger of the amber liquid remained at the bottom.

"Thanks." Trey looked at each of his oldest and dearest friends and his usually disorganized but steadfast younger brother. He couldn't imagine getting married without every one of them here to support him. In the end, after months of stressing about wedding plans, surviving what had felt like a summer of never-ending setbacks, and the outright calamities occurring left and right, he and Tania had settled on the perfect number for their wedding party.

The guys hoisted their drinks. Heath toasted, "It's been a wild summer, but you and Tania were meant to be." Heath echoed the sentiments rooted deep in Trey's heart. "I doubt there's one person attending this wedding who doesn't agree with me. You and Tania complement each other in the best ways. You steady her, and she stands by you no matter what. That includes needing to organize opening your consulting business years before you expected, on the heels of the Great Whitaker Organic Farms Extended Family Meltdown. Come this October, watch out, organic-farming world! Here comes my big bro."

Ren lifted his glass high. "Here, here."

Heath smiled. "Tania's gonna be an amazing wife. And a great mom, when that day comes. I already know you're a fantastic brother, Trey. So, I can state unequivocally that you'll make an incredible husband and, eventually, a great father." Heath wiped a tear from the corner of one eye. "In fact, after years of enjoying my single-dude status, it's hard to believe I'm saying this, but I might be jealous."

The Pike boys and Ren laughed. Keon smiled, glancing down at his glass and shaking his head.

Trey said, "I swear, sometimes I didn't know if this day would come."

"But the day is here," Keon responded, "and the ceremony is at hand. Let's get you hitched."

Adrenaline coursed through Trey's veins. "You're gonna know what this feels like in a year or so," he said to Keon, who gave another wide smile.

"You and my brothers will coach me through it."

Trey nodded. The guys cheered, and the group tossed back their scotches.

Closing his eyes, Trey breathed in and out through his nostrils. The wedding-themed speaker above the door chimed. His attendants filed into the hall and turned toward the chapel.

Heath signaled Trey to follow him out the door. "It's now or never, brother."

Trey swallowed. This was it. The last moments of his single life.

He smiled at his brother. "It's now."

Chapter Seven

Breathing exercises were for the birds, Tania decided. Despite months of practicing mindful inhalations, her nerves quaked, and a heightened sense of drama permeated the antechamber to the blueberry farm's rustic wedding chapel. Her stomach knotted as she cocked an ear for her cue to proceed down the aisle. Only minutes remained until she married the man of her dreams. *Trey*. So why did the prospect of accomplishing the deed loom in her mind like a long-fought-for and unattainable goal?

Her mom and bridesmaids flitted around the vestibule. Touching up her hair. Checking her makeup. Adjusting the train of her snug-to-the-knees mermaid-style wedding gown. The beaded lace weighed down her bodice, and her pulse scattered like tossed confetti.

What had convinced her the extravagant dress design suited her tiny frame? And who had dreamed up the literally *too*-bright idea of selecting five different colors for the bridesmaid dresses? The 'sunset hues' Tania had considered romantic two weeks earlier at the bridal boutique blinded her every time she blinked.

The profiles of her attendants and the bouquets waving around obscured her view beyond the last three rows of chapel chairs. Her jitters skated along a narrow precipice as the cute-as-kittens flower girl and ring bearer trundled into the assembly of friends and family. The notes of the processional carried to Tania's ears as the children suddenly raced down the aisle. Gleeful giggles echoed off the high ceilings.

Peering ahead, Tania glimpsed Mina's basket of rose petals tumbling to the floor. Several guests tittered, and a pit sank in her stomach. Had Leo managed to hold on to the ring pillow?

She craned her neck, attempting to catch a better look. No luck.

Fighting the urge to chew off her lipstick, she wrinkled her forehead. "Mom, those poor kids. Why are people laughing?"

"It's all right," Mom responded in a soothing tone. "The tykes are jacked up on sugar. Why your cousin stuffed them full of gummy bears during the drive from Rosewood is beyond me."

Tania winced. "Maybe we should have kept with tradition." The abundance of wedding websites described that child attendants headed to the altar after the maid of honor and before the bride and the bride's father. Or, in this case, the bride and her mom. But the preschoolers were tuckered from the fifty-minute car ride to the Carnation area, which, under usual traffic conditions, took thirty-five. A rusted pickup had careened into a ditch, creating the delay. Tania's cousin requested the change to the processional once her family arrived safely at the farm. Tania hadn't had it in her to insist on the same order as if the wedding had occurred in Rosewood.

"It doesn't matter," Mom murmured, grazing Tania's forearm with calming fingertips. "You're marrying Trey. That's what counts."

Tania rested a hand on the lace covering her tummy. Another month into her likely pregnancy and she might not have fit into her dress! In hindsight, her wedding diet hadn't been responsible for the extra lost pounds. Her and Trey's maybe-baby had soaked up every ounce of nourishment she'd put into her mouth this summer. She gulped.

"You're right," she said, breathing a mite easier. "I need to stay focused on the prize." Marrying Trey.

Noni cast a sympathetic glance from her position near the entry into the chapel. She peered inside. "The pillow is intact," she reported over her shoulder.

"Thanks." Tania kissed her fingertips and waved them toward her youngest sister. The rings sewn onto the satin cushion Leo carried were replicas. Heath, as their best man, transported the real wedding bands in his tuxedo pocket. After the chaos of this summer, Tania supposed a dumped basket of rose petals wasn't a big deal.

Claire lowered onto the floor beside Tania's hip and repositioned the sweep train. "Can you move a few inches to the left?" her maid of honor asked.

"Oh. Right." Glancing down, Tania followed Claire's instructions.

Mom leaned close. "Noni is partway down the aisle," Mom whispered. "And there goes Tami."

Tania's vision blurred. Claire had distracted her

with the business of the train, but in seconds *her* turn to face the wedding music would arrive.

Was she ready?

Mouth drying, she faced forward. The soles of her feet prickled in the bridesmaid sandals Mom had confiscated from Tami. The sensation felt weirdly like when Tania's toes lifted off the earth during a stress dream. She needed an anchor before she floated away!

"It's time," Janie whispered, handing Tania a cascading bouquet of thorn-clipped roses, peonies, and assorted greenery. Tania gripped the ribbon-wrapped stems tighter than an angler reeling in a forty-pound salmon. Janie instructed, "Hold your wrist at your hip. People want to see your face, not the flowers."

Tania lowered the bouquet with another arid gulp as Janie turned and entered the chapel, Alicia on her heels.

"Help," Tania beseeched Claire, who smiled and chuckled. Sure, her best friend wasn't the one getting married. *Yet.*

"You've got this," Claire whispered in the split-second before she entered the chapel.

"Mom," Tania squeaked. "I don't know if I can move my feet."

Her mom clasped her clammy hand. "Sweetheart, you're on the verge of an incredible life with Trey. Nerves are natural. Except..." Mom paused. "Only *you* know what is in your heart. If you've changed your mind and don't want to get married today—or on any day—it's better Trey finds out now." Mom placed a tender kiss on Tania's cheek. "Even if the news hurts him, you're my daughter. I want you to make the decision that's best for you."

Certainty washed over her shoulders. "I want to marry Trey. But I'm so nervous." And queasy again. Where were her crackers?

"I've never been prouder of you than I am at this moment," Mom said, dashing away a tear. "Trey organized a small surprise for you at the altar. That's probably why Mina dropped her basket. The child couldn't contain her excitement. Although, those darn gummy bears..."

Panic building, Tania nodded. Earlier, at the house, Trey had mentioned a surprise. She'd assumed he was referring to a present for their wedding night. What in the world could he have arranged to happen *now*? He wasn't holding a sign announcing she maybe-carried his baby, was he?

Because they hadn't discussed that possibility. At all.

The strains of the bridal chorus amplified, and the voice of the minister carried into the vestibule as Esther asked the assembly to stand. Clothing rustled. Footwear shuffled. The blood swooshed out of Tania's face.

"Whatever *you* decide," Mom emphasized, meeting her gaze. "I'm sorry you couldn't do this with your father as well." Sadness traced Mom's smile.

Emotion lodged a lump in Tania's throat. "I didn't want Dad for my walk. I want you. And Trey. I want Trey." The man she trusted with her heart. The father of her unborn child. *Her* TLT.

Mom smiled. "Then let's go."

Tania nodded as tunnel vision reduced her world to scant inches in front of her feet. Gripping her mom's arm, she stepped forward.

"You're doing it," Mom whispered. "We're walking." The pressure of Mom's fingertips increased on her forearm. "Sweetheart, open your eyes. Look toward your man. We'll head in his direction. It's as simple as that."

Tania's eyelids quivered open. When had she closed them?

She pasted on a gracious bridal persona, glancing at a cousin and then an uncle as she and her mom strolled between the standing guests. Huge dots materialized in front of her eyes, and her breath threatened to vacate her lungs. She couldn't make out Trey over the visual impact of the multitude. She trained her gaze on the hand-hewn altar. She breathed in. She breathed out.

Oh! Her heart lifted. There! She spotted him!

A smile brightened his handsome face. He motioned a thumb toward her bridesmaids, and her eyes rounded.

"*Teacup*?" Tania whispered, following the path of her nearly-husband's gestures. Alicia, standing in the row of bridesmaids, gripped two rhinestone-encrusted leashes. Spats, Alicia's old dachshund, wearing a black-and-white doggie tuxedo, snoozed at her feet. Teacup, Tania and Trey's Yorkie, perched at attention between Mina and Leo. The children sat cross-legged in front of the bridesmaids and on either side of the animals. Teacup sported a poofy canine bridal outfit smudged with dirt, as if the pupper had rolled around on the ground at the first opportunity.

Chuckles and murmurs rose from their guests as Tania drank in the sight of Trey's sweet and thoughtful surprise.

"Mom," she whispered. "How did he...?"

"Aren't the dogs cute?" Mom whispered back. "Trey Whitaker is one of a kind. Everyone you love is here to support you, Tania. Your father is watching the livestream, offering his blessing on the marriage in his own way."

By staying out of *her* way, Tania concluded. She gave a quick nod. She couldn't spend more energy on her father's efforts. Not when thoughts of Trey flooded her heart and gushed happiness through her veins.

Her nearly-husband's gaze locked on hers, and joyous tears dampened her eyes. Her sisters and their closest friends stood on either side of the altar. Claire and Janie wiped their cheeks. Esther, the minister from Rosewood Community Church, smiled behind the podium.

Trey crooked a finger toward the first row of guests. Tania's eyes grew huge when the dog-sitter they'd hired late last week clicked a device, snapping both dogs to attention.

The woman delivered each pup a treat. The woman accepted the leashes from Alicia and escorted the weirdly well-mannered dogs toward an outside door at the rear of the chapel.

Tania's heart melted as Mina and Leo scampered behind the dog-sitter. The kids' mom completed the merry troupe as the group exited the chapel to a cloudy but pleasant day outside.

Tania handed her bouquet to Claire. Facing Trey, Tania clasped his hands. "Thank you," she whispered, throat tight. "You are the most thoughtful man."

"Anything for my TLT," he responded in a husky voice also tinged with sentiment. "Heath took our unruly Teacup to wedding-dog lessons," he whispered.

"You mean the woman boarding Teacup during our honeymoon is a dog trainer?" Tania asked in a soft voice. "Wow. Thank you so much." That they had reorganized dog-care arrangements suddenly made a lot more sense.

Trey nodded. "You look beautiful," he whispered.

"I love you," she replied, choking up again.

At the podium, Esther chuckled. "We skipped a part."

Tania's cheeks warmed. She glanced at her mom, standing a foot behind them. "Oh, no. You're supposed to give me away. I'm sorry, Mom."

"It works this way too," Esther said. She asked Mom, "Who gives Tania in marriage to Trey?"

"I do," Mom responded in a proud voice. "I am

beyond ecstatic that this fine young man is about to become my son-in-law."

Esther's smile broadened. "That little addition wasn't in the script either," she said, and the assembly laughed. "It seems we're winging this ceremony today." Esther's gaze swept over the congregation. "Please sit."

As Tania's mom and their guests took their seats, Esther's glance settled first on Trey and then Tania. Esther opened the monogrammed wedding folder. She cleared her throat. "Marriage offers permanence and structure to the love a couple feels for each other," she began. "This afternoon, in front of family and friends, Trey and Tania—"

Tania's hand popped up. "Wait."

"What is it?" Trey whispered, love and concern palpable in his gaze and voice.

Tania glanced at Esther. "I have something to say."

The minister's head tilted. "We rehearsed a traditional ceremony at the church last night."

"Yes, but so much has happened." Heart pounding, Tania looked at Trey again. She gripped his fingers. "Trey," she said, voice trembling. "Our vows might be conventional, but the love I feel for you is anything but. I can't help saying something now. And I want everyone to hear me."

A sheen glossed his eyes. "Go ahead," he whispered roughly.

She drew in a long breath. "Janie introduced us." She glanced over at her dear friend in the row of bridesmaids.

"You mean she set you up?" Claire quipped, and a chuckle rippled throughout the chapel.

Janie shrugged. "When you know a couple belongs together, you know."

Tania smiled at her two best friends. Then she returned her gaze to Trey. Her heart skipped a happy beat. "It's true that if not for Janie noticing me noticing *you*, honey, four years ago at the state fairgrounds, she might not have faked stubbing her toe —" Emotion clogged her throat yet again. She paused.

He picked up the slack, describing the evening. "The *fake* toe-stubbing conveniently prevented her from boarding the Ferris wheel with you." He smiled.

Swallowing tears of happiness, Tania nodded. "Janie vouched for you as her stand-in, saying you and she went way back—"

"When, in fact, we'd met twenty minutes earlier

in the lineup for popcorn." Trey directed his gaze at their guests. "Janie and I talked in line," he explained, "and I asked if this lovely lady"—his fingers tightened on Tania's—"was seeing anyone. Luckily, she wasn't." His gaze settled on Tania again. "I thought you were the most beautiful woman I'd ever seen. I still do. You're beautiful inside and out."

Whispers and murmurings of approval lifted from the crowd, and Tania mustered the bravery to continue. "As soon as I saw *you*, Trey...the very first moment our gazes met...my heart felt like it actually leaped in my chest. I didn't know such a thing was physically possible. I thought people made up stuff like that. As it turns out, my heart can leap."

"So can mine," he whispered, thumbs brushing her knuckles. "It does every day we're together."

She blinked away the dampness coating her eyelashes. "Because of Janie's fake stubbed toe, you offered to ride the Ferris wheel with me. So, I guess you could say she introduced us. Or she set us up. I'm fine with whatever our friends and family want to call it. Because I am *thrilled* that Janie faked an injury. Trey, I love Ferris wheels, but I get scared when the car stops at the top. You hugged me and made sure I was okay. My heart became yours in that moment, and we have been together since." Her voice quieted with every sentence, but she forged on. "I love you, Trey Whitaker. The last four years have been incredible, and I want them to continue being amazing. With everything in my heart. Years and years and years ahead of us, my love. For the rest of our lives. No matter what happens, I promise to stand by you. To stand *with* you."

"I'll stand with *you*," he whispered, releasing one of her hands to dab moisture from his eyes.

"Well," Esther stated. "This ceremony has taken on a life of its own."

Tania glanced toward the minister and asked, "May we continue?"

Esther swept out a hand. "By all means."

Tania looked at her nearly-husband. He gathered her hands into his larger ones.

"Life can feel scary and full of unknowns," Tania said, gazing at Trey. "I'm not always the easiest person to live with. I can get in my own way. I've gotten in *our* way, believing I didn't deserve a man as caring and thoughtful as you have proven to be, time and again." She choked back a fresh onslaught of overwhelming love. "But I *do* deserve you, Trey. I deserve your love and support, and you deserve mine. Babe, you're stuck with me."

Although her words didn't sound romantic to

her ears, a collective sigh lifted from their friends and family.

Tania said, "Every surprising event that occurred this summer showed, over and over, that you will be an amazing husband. *My* amazing husband, Trey. And you'll be a fantastic father to our babies." She wet her lips. "Trey Whitaker, from this day forward, I promise to stand by you. To stand with you. I love you, Trey. I do." She whipped her gaze to Esther's. *"Oops."*

Esther shrugged. "I can't say I've officiated a wedding where the couple says 'I Do' before the ceremony starts, but there's always a first time." She indicated Trey. "The legal and traditional vows can come after you speak your heart."

He nodded. "Sweetheart," he said, looking at Tania. She fell more deeply in love with him as his gaze captured hers and he added in a tender tone, "Who wouldn't fall in love with you?" He smiled, and her tummy flipped. "I didn't stand a chance, and I wouldn't have it any other way. That day at the fairgrounds was meant to be. I need you to understand that. We were *meant to be,*" he murmured, and the words wove beneath her ribs. Curled around her heart. "The universe smiled upon us. And now, Tania Hoyt, I get to be your husband.

Do you understand how blessed I feel? I have the privilege of being the father of the first of our babies." His eyebrows twitched, and he let slip a secretive smile. "To every baby who joins our family."

The congregation sighed. Some happy sobs echoed off the chapel ceiling, and Tania's certainty about loving Trey—trusting him to stand by her—dug deep into her soul. The corners of her mouth quivered as she smiled.

"I consider myself the luckiest man," he said. "I'll forever be grateful to Janie for fake-stubbing her toe. To meet a woman for the very first time—to meet *you*, Tania—and be filled with an understanding, a rightness, a surety, that you are the person I was meant to share my life with? That's remarkable. That's a lifelong love."

Tears brimmed over Tania's lashes and heated her cheeks as he added, "I promise we will grow in our lives as partners. I choose to be your husband today and every day. I'll strive to be the best dad possible as we raise our family. To understand in the deepest part of my heart that when hard times hit—and we know they will—we will fight our way *through* them. Together. That is my wish for today and for all our days. I love you, Tania, and I want you to be my wife. Like really soon." He curved the back of his hand in a tender caress against her cheek. He whispered, "I do."

"I want you to be my husband," Tania whispered. "I do."

Esther spread her palms. "Go ahead and kiss your bride, Trey. Then we'll start."

Epilogue

End of September
Fourteen months later

"All settled?" the cheerful flight attendant asked.

"Getting there," Trey responded with a smile. He dug in the diaper backpack at his feet for his baby girl's favorite teething toy.

Nodding, the woman turned her gaze toward Tania and their adorable six-month-old, Abigail Beatrice. The baby squirmed on her mama's lap in the window seat. "Do you need anything?" the woman asked Tania.

Tania glanced at the attendant. "No, thank you.

We're content." She pinned her gaze on Abby's animated expression. "For now," she added in a goofy voice.

The flight attendant nodded and moved down the aisle.

Trey watched as Tania scrunched her nose and waggled her eyebrows at their baby. Abby squealed in delight, drool dribbling from her cherub lips as she reached her chubby arms toward her mama. His wife.

His wife. The words unspooled in his brain, and a satisfying warmth spread deep inside his chest. Tania was his wife. Abigail was his daughter. They were a family. He loved everything about his life right now, but these two were his world.

Tania exchanged a look with him. Their good friends Janie McAllister and Keon Rivers were getting married the day after tomorrow. Janie's Seattle-area family and friends had booked every spot on the turbo-prop plane. Which meant Trey and Tania were familiar with everyone boarding. Lucky thing. While the flight from Sea-Tac to Kelowna International Airport in British Columbia took seventy-two minutes, the ascent and descent would likely cause the baby's ears discomfort. As a precaution, they'd packed a bottle of expressed breast milk, two pacifiers, a rattle, and Abby's giraffe teether. He handed the toy to Abby. The baby rewarded him with a cutely crooked grin, exposing her first tooth, cut last week.

Tania's phone chimed a notification for an incoming text.

"Shoot. It's my dad."

Trey inhaled. Fourteen months ago, his mother-in-law commandeered the phones of the wedding party to corral rumors of the commotion her ex-husband wrought that morning. What a godsend. For a few days, wedding guests outside of immediate friends and family hadn't realized Boldt had swept into town with an ill-conceived plan to transform his daughter's wedding into a publicity stunt for his latest—and ultimately last—country music single.

Understandably, Bea had only contained the situation to a degree. Without knowledge of the events that transpired at the house, dozens of wedding guests captured the ceremony on their devices. Plus, the videographer recorded the livestream that fed to Boldt's hotel room. After two weeks of camping off-grid, Trey and Tania returned to Rosewood to learn their premature wedding vows had gone viral throughout Greater Seattle. When the blueberry farm requested permission to highlight the best clips to the new events center website advertising wedding services, Tania and Trey agreed. They'd owed the Bonners for helping them pull off their big day.

Now, on the plane, Abby's eyelids drooped closed. The teether slowly slipped from the baby's grip as her head relaxed against her mama's shoulder. Trey caught the toy and placed it on his lap. He kissed the wispy red-gold curls on his daughter's sweet-smelling head.

He whispered to Tania, "Are you okay?"

"Yeah." She sighed. "I'm willing to give Boldt a chance, but it'll take time to establish any real level of trust."

Trey caressed the knuckles of her closest hand.

Tania murmured, "He's stayed out of the limelight since the fundraisers for rebuilding the church. I'll give him that." She planted a quick kiss on Abby's plump cheek.

"What did his message say?"

She showed him her phone, and he read:

> You three enjoy yourselves.

Tania sighed. "I'm surprised he remembered we're going away. He's been so busy."

"And restrained." Considering the man's expressive personality, Trey thought.

A faint glimmer of good humor sparkled in Tania's eyes. "He's lucky he didn't find himself under a restraining order after what he pulled. The least he can do is *act* restrained. If by that, you mean he seems to have learned how to exhibit a tiny bit of self-control."

A smile tugged Trey's mouth, and pride bloomed within him at the thought of the progress his wife and her father had made in the ten months since Boldt had moved to the Puget Sound. Three weeks post-wedding, Boldt wrote individual emails to each of his daughters, stating that the day's events had bopped him on the head like Maxwell Silver's hammer from the old Beatles' song. Boldt chronicled how his daughters' understandably upset responses to his surprise appearance woke him up to the damage he'd caused them over a lifetime of neglect. Twenty years.

"Are you texting him back?" he asked.

"I haven't decided." Stroking their daughter's cuddly body with one hand, she thumb-scrolled through her phone with the other.

Trey massaged his wife's shoulder, offering his support without speaking. The past year had been a mainly happy but activity-filled blur, he mused as he drank in the curve of her face.

His gaze drifted to their daughter's rosy cheek, and his chest warmed. Last October, he launched his organic-farming consulting firm to success, for which he was grateful. Around the same time, Tania's dad bought a house in North Seattle and began a new career as a freelance alt-country-music producer.

Boldt worked out of a recording studio in Phinney Ridge. Amidst the massive changes and the man's many apologies to his daughters, upon his return, the musician vowed to stay out of their lives until—and if—any of them felt ready to allow him back in. Then, he had said, he would welcome the opportunity.

He'd also pledged not to step on Bea's toes—and not to trample Whitaker grandparenting rights—regarding any role he might play in Abigail's life. For that, Trey felt grateful.

At first, Tania wanted nothing to do with her father. Noni and Tami made tentative steps toward including him in their lives. In a way, the younger Hoyt women acted as test subjects for their pregnant and therefore more vulnerable older sister. Then, when the three Hoyt women—one now carrying the Whitaker surname—committed to fundraising for the rebuilding of Rosewood Community Church, Tania spotted a window to evaluate her father's new-leaf philosophies.

A surge of admiration rose in Trey's throat as he recalled her bravery and resolve. Her father wanted to atone for his sins of the past? Then he was free to jump through hoops to prove he deserved that chance. Tania invited him to perform free of charge at three concerts she and other members of the fundraising committee arranged for the reconstruction of the church and hall.

The challenge for Boldt was two-fold. One, pulling in the largest audiences possible without too much fanfare and, two, performing his ass off without embarrassing his daughters or his ex-wife.

The man had delivered the best performances of his life. All without belting out one note of his greatest hit, *She's Got Great Gams*, or strumming a single chord of, *It's a Pity*.

Thereafter, Tania and her dad formed a tenuous alliance. Since Abigail's birth, Tania had felt comfortable enough to permit Boldt a monthly visit.

Trey massaged her shoulder again. "Babe?" he asked in an encouraging tone.

She chewed her lip. "I'll let Mom know we're on board."

"Here, I'll take Abby while you do," he said, cradling Abigail's snuggly body against his chest. The baby nestled into the crook of his neck, and he breathed in her sweet scent.

Tania looked up from her phone as the plane slowly filled. "Mom is okay with me texting Dad," she half-whispered.

Trey sympathized with his mother-in-law. Boldt's return had been tough on Bea, although the situation grew easier with each passing month, especially now that Bea was dating someone she'd met at the fundraisers. Still, these were Tania's waters to negotiate.

"I realize it's up to me," she whispered. A shadow passed over her eyes. "So does Mom. It's hard to let go of the hurt Dad inflicted. I want to support her."

Trey kissed her cheek. Quietly, he said, "I'll support *you* however you need."

She released a sigh. "It's a lot. Dad is trying, but I hope for everyone's sake he doesn't cave under the pressure of hopefully becoming a better human being."

"Fair point. If he caves, we'll deal. But...he's given you the lead on his relationship with you and with Abby. He's done everything he said he would."

Tania gazed at Abigail. A wistful expression graced her lips. "I want our daughter to have a relationship with both her grandfathers. To be honest, I'm terrified Boldt will leave again. I don't want him popping in and out of her life, like a puppet at a street fair. I want her to know she can count on him."

"We'll keep taking things slow," Trey reassured his wife as they each nuzzled the baby.

Another incoming text dinged on Tania's phone. She giggled and held the screen toward him. He read the message from his father-in-law.

> Bang, bang, Maxwell's silver hammer.

"Cute," Trey quipped.

Tania pursed her lips. *Thanks, Dad*, she typed. She looked at Trey. "He hasn't asked about Abby."

"Maybe he doesn't want to push."

"It's been three weeks since he saw her."

"He'll see her after we get back. Don't worry, babe. He'll survive."

She inhaled. "I want to send him a picture."

"Of the baby? Are you sure?"

She nodded and aimed the phone at their napping child. Another moment later, she sent the photo to Boldt. Sucking in a breath, she continued holding the phone between herself and Trey. A message from her father slid onto the screen.

Thank you, Tania. She's beautiful.

Tania smiled and put the phone into airplane mode before tucking the device into her purse. "Come here, baby," she said, reaching for Abby. Trey passed over their daughter, who roused and blinked drowsily. Drool dribbled down Abby's chin. Trey cleaned the moisture with a soft cloth.

"I'm proud of you," he whispered to Tania as she cuddled their daughter. He kissed the baby's cheek and said, "We're going to be okay."

Tania nodded, gaze twinkling. "We *are* good together."

"We are incredible." They were the partners Trey had visualized when he'd proposed. The months before their wedding had been tumultuous, but

Tania was the woman of his dreams, and she was blossoming before his eyes.

"I love you," he whispered, giving her a quick kiss.

"I love you," she whispered against his lips.

In the row ahead of them, Heath groaned. Trey's brother peered through the sliver of space between the two headrests. "All right, all right," Heath joked. "Save it for the hotel room." He goggled at the baby. "What do you say, Abby-baby?"

"Gah," the baby declared. Abigail dug a finger into her open mouth, poking the digit at her exposed tooth.

"You're the best," Heath responded, tapping his own front teeth in response. "Try not to scream in my ear during the flight, okay? Direct every ounce of displeasure toward your dad." He winked at the baby.

Abigail reached toward her uncle. Heath blew her a kiss, then turned back around.

Trey passed the baby the giraffe teether. She stuffed one of the toy's soft hooves into her mouth.

At the front of the plane, the second flight attendant addressed the passengers while the airline employee who had spoken to Trey and Tania performed a last check of the rows.

"We hear there's a wedding up in Canada this weekend," the young male attendant said into a handset, projecting his voice. "And everyone onboard is attending."

Cheers erupted from the youngest and rowdiest passengers, seated in the last rows. Abigail's eyes rounded. She waved her teether and screeched with happiness. A cacophony of laughter sounded from surrounding passengers.

"Great," Tania mumbled, shushing the baby. "She has an audience."

"She'll settle down," Trey said as Abigail squirmed and gnawed her toy.

Tania smiled. "What makes you think that?"

"Because you're the best," Trey whispered in his wife's ear as their fellow passengers quieted. "The best wife, and also the best mother."

"*We're* the best," she whispered, kissing his cheek and then Abigail's. "And the best of the rest of our lives is yet to come."

Trey locked eyes with his wife over the wispy-soft hair crowning their baby's head.

"The best is already here," he said, squeezing her hand as the plane rumbled down the runway.

Acknowledgments

Thank you once more to Mary J. Forbes for her gracious reading of the first draft of *Trusting Trey*.

I've known for years that I wanted to write a story where the church burns to a crisp. How would a couple deal with that stress? The idea had its beginnings in the church for my own wedding burning down a few months afterward. In our case, the fire was set on purpose (not us!), but the memories of our beautiful wedding day persevere regardless. My husband and I have now been married for 40 years! Thank you, Steve, for remaining my steadfast partner throughout the many challenges we have faced over four decades. 🤍

About the Author

Cindy Procter-King writes steamy romcoms and contemporary romances bursting with laughter and emotion. Sassy feel-good fiction!

Cindy's books are available from eBook retailers all over the world, as well as in trade paperback, some library hardcover and large print, and some foreign editions.

Cindy lives in Canada with her family, Ghost'Da Allie McBeagle, and too many grand-dogs to count!

For more on Cindy's books, visit:
www.cindyprocter-king.com

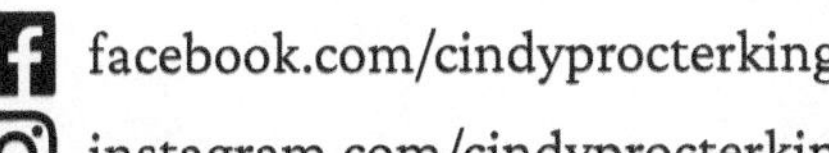

facebook.com/cindyprocterkingauthor

instagram.com/cindyprocterking

bookbub.com/authors/cindy-procter-king

x.com/cindypk

Crave another sassy romance?

www.readsassyromance.com

www.ingramcontent.com/pod-product-compliance
Lightning Source LLC
Chambersburg PA
CBHW031055310726
48969CB00007B/2283